ECHOES OF LOVE

Sara Farrow jumped at the chance of a job in the South of France, writing the history of the Lorivel parfumerie. Even the unfriendly reception from her devastatingly handsome boss, Paul Merinard, couldn't dampen her enthusiasm. But why did the old housekeeper in the shuttered house dislike Sara so much that she tried to kill her, and why, oh why, did Paul distrust her motives when the very sight of him made her heart beat so fast?

ECHOES OF LOVE

CHAPTER ONE

'Sara,' Mr Gaunt said from the doorway of her small office, 'You speak French, don't you?'

He might have been standing there for some moments, watching her as she sat in a dream. Sara, trying to suppress a jump as she collected herself from her none-too-happy thoughts, looked up at him guiltily, flushing a little with the childish tell-tale colour which *would* creep up her cheeks at the least excuse. Not that Mr Gaunt was the type to criticise her for doing nothing, despite being the head of the firm and her boss: in fact he treated her with paternal kindness, and she had been 'Sara' rather than 'Miss Farrow' from the first moment she had arrived in the office some eight months ago.

'Yes, Mr Gaunt,' she said now, trying to sound alert, and pulling her shoulders up quickly from their miserable droop. It was bad enough to feel both foolish and unhappy, without making such a public thing of it that everyone, right up to the head of the firm, could see it.

'Fluently, I believe?' he pressed.

'What?' Oh, the French, of course. 'Yes—I was at school in Paris, at an ordinary French lycée. When I lived there with my grandfather.' Carl Farrow, though a widower, had brought her up after her parent's death, making time for her in his busy musician's life so that she should have the security of a home and unquestioned belonging. Sara tried to make her voice sound less distracted and more efficient as she asked, 'Is there something which needs translating?'

'Not exactly. I've had a request which might interest you. You haven't any ties, I believe? Any reason why you particularly want to stay in London?'

'I haven't any family. But London is—is the place to be if you want to be a writer, isn't it?' With a bright spot of colour on each cheek, Sara gazed at Mr Gaunt with the sudden horrified idea that he might be giving her the sack. She had never hidden the fact that she had come to work for a publishing firm because she wanted to be a writer—but surely she hadn't been doing her job here as a junior editor that badly? And Mr Gaunt had been nothing but encouraging about the stories she wrote in her spare time; he had even had someone from the fiction side of the business read some of her work and advise her, and had congratulated her when she sold two of her stories and an article.

Or—oh horrors—had he decided to sack her because he knew how stupidly she'd fallen for the charms of his top assistant, Dennis Mather, and found the whole thing embarrassing? Surely they had been more private than that (extremely private, as it turned out, because Dennis had had a fiancée all the time whom he had no intention of losing). And, on his side at least, it hadn't amounted to more than a lightly deliberate pursuit which took in a dinner-date or two and some very expert kisses. With mingled shame and bitterness, Sara felt quite sure that Dennis had already forgotten the whole thing.

She turned her attention to Mr Gaunt once more. 'Of course it is,' he replied, 'but I'm not asking you to leave London for good. I thought you might like to work abroad for a spell. Or don't you feel ready for that sort of responsibility?' he added, mistaking her look of surprise for reluctance.

Her chin went up, stubbornly. 'If there's a job you want me to do,' she assured Mr Gaunt firmly, 'I'm sure I can do it!'

'So am I, or I wouldn't be talking to you about it. You are interested, then? Good. Come into my office and we'll talk about it properly.'

Half an hour later Sara, a little dazed, found she had agreed to all sorts of things. So far from giving her the sack, and with no mention of Dennis at all, Mr Gaunt seemed to be offering her an exciting opportunity. She found herself agreeing that yes, she could go to the South of France at short notice. Yes, she was fluent enough to work in both French and English, since she was more or less bilingual; and no, she didn't mind the idea of

12

helping an old man assemble his memories. The old man in question was called James Halberson, and he was English, though he had lived in France for many years. She would be expected to live in the house with him and his housekeeper, and since the old man was sometimes in frail health, her hours of work would probably be variable. She must be able to drive, and there would be a car for her use. As for the work itself, Mr Gaunt warned, it would be factual rather than imaginative, though there *would* be a human angle. Mr Halberson wanted to write the history of the firm he had worked for for many years, the Parfumerie Lorivel; but with it he would have to include some of the history of the Merinard family. The Merinards *were* Lorivel, from its original founding right up to the present day, so could not be left out.

'James Halberson's niece married Jacques Merinard,' Mr Gaunt explained, 'and Halberson went to France to work for the firm after living in the Far East. Perhaps he had some knowledge of exotic plants to offer, and he had a scientific training. Lorivel certainly produced some very striking new perfumes around that time. Have you heard of them?'

'Oh yes. Very exclusive, and very, very expensive. Nothing I could ever afford! A bit—a bit heavy for my taste anyway.' Sara was beginning to feel a sparkle of excitement as the whole project caught her interest. 'They're very French—I don't think they sell so much in England. Aren't they at Grasse, where the other famous perfume factories are?'

'Yes, near Grasse, though Lorivel is much smaller than the big perfumeries, and still very much a family concern. But Halberson lives further south still, on the coast—the Corniche l'Esterel. Do you know that part of France?' As Sara shook her head, Mr Gaunt gave an appreciative sigh. 'It's one of the most beautiful coastlines in Europe. I wouldn't mind going there myself—particularly now, before the tourist season gets under way! Apart from the occasional mistral, it should be getting warm there now—unlike here!' He gave a rueful glance at the grey March sky outside the window, with rain spattering on a cold wind, 'Although you'll be working, you should get the chance to see something of the countryside. I envy you. I don't usually find ghost writers for people,' he added, giving Sara his kindly smile, 'but it occurred to me that you deserve the chance. Mind you, I can only make the suggestion, so it isn't a promise! I'll cable them tonight and see what they say.'

'It's very nice of you—'

He waved that way, glancing at the letter in front of him on the desk, then looking back at Sara with a twinkle. 'I gather they want something to keep the old man safely in retirement and out of everyone's hair. You'll be adequately paid on top of your living expenses—and we'll keep a job open for you here, of course, if you want one. But, who knows—you might find you've collected some background material for that novel you want to write, and decide to concentrate on that!'

It sounded almost too good to be true, but when Sara tried to stammer her thanks, he waved them away again, adding, as if as an afterthought, that it would be 'quite a good time for her to be out of the office.' For a second, Sara knew another moment's doubt.

Was he sending her away because of Dennis? His look of bland innocence denied anything of the sort, and reassured her.

Caution reminded her that she hadn't actually got the job yet, but even so she was bubbling over with the idea when she went home that evening and let herself into her flat. She must talk to her flatmate about it, of course, and check that the other girl didn't mind being left in charge of the apartment when—if—Sara went away. Betty was engaged to an engineer at present working abroad, but he wasn't due back for another year, so she wouldn't have any immediate moving plans herself.

'Bet?' She burst into the living-room with her excitement showing in her face, however hard she tried to suppress it. 'You'll never guess what's happened—'

'Your "office wolf's" back on the scene again?' Betty asked drily, looking up from the newspaper she was reading. Catching Sara's startled expression, she had the grace to look rueful. 'Sorry, I shouldn't have said that, should I? It's not my business, but—'

16

'I didn't know you thought of him like that!'

'Well I do. He's a type. I wanted to say something before, but I didn't think you'd take it too kindly! But you've been looking so miserable lately that I felt like kicking him! No, Sara, I *will* say it, even if you don't want to listen! He's a super-smoothy with good looks and a lot of conscious charm, and I'd imagine he goes round breaking hearts because it builds up his ego. There, I've had my say, and you can throw something at me if you like! But I just couldn't sit there and watch you being so—so *vulnerable*; and *I* think it's a pity your Dennis ever came back from America at all, so there!'

'*Not* my Dennis,' Sara said mildly, 'he turns out to be engaged to someone else. The daughter of the American firm he was working in, as a matter of fact.' It had been a remarkably forthright speech from the normally placid Betty, and one which had surprised her: the two girls took some care not to interfere in each other's lives. 'No, it's all right, I'm not cross! But I'm stronger than you think I am, you know. I must be: he hasn't even crossed my mind for the past hour!' This, remarkably, was true. 'So much for a broken heart,' Sara said lightly, to hide a remembering pang. 'No, this is something else. A job! I might be going to France!'

As she told Bet all about it, excitement caught her again. The two girls discussed it, particularly the famous Lorivel Parfumerie which, as Betty pointed out, could scarcely prove dull to any female. The flat was no problem, Betty assured Sara. When they reached the point of working out exactly when Sara might have to leave, Sara called a halt; she hadn't, she reminded both of them, actually *got* the job yet. It might never happen.

'Well, *if* it doesn't...you *will* still avoid the "office wolf", won't you?' Betty asked, sobering into a concern which showed in her eyes.

'I've told you, that's over. I can't help avoiding him at the moment: he's gone to Amsterdam to a Book Fair. Let's not discuss it—I just made an idiot of myself, that's all.' To lighten the mood, Sara threw a cushion at her friend, and said with mock fierceness, 'And I am *not* vulnerable, whatever you mean

18

by that! People fall in and out of love all the time, and I'm no exception. It's all part of life—except for sober engaged ladies like you, of course!'

'Hm. *Have* you ever been in love? Seriously? Say, to the point of living with someone?'

'Not actually to the point of living with someone.' Sara felt as if she was flushing under Bet's scrutiny, and went on quickly, 'But I *have* been in love *very* seriously,' she said impishly, 'when I was fifteen I was in love with a Rumanian violinist. It was because he was the most beautiful man I'd ever met. He really was beautiful, too—very dark hair and high cheekbones and deep romantic brown eyes—'

'I meant really!'

'Of course it was real! He was about thirty-five. He hardly spoke to me, of course, because his French was awful and his English was even worse. But he used to manage "hello" and smile at me—and I adored him. He was first violin in my grandfather's orchestra at the time.' Sara gave a small chuckle at the memory. 'I'd forgotten all about him until now! So you see—I'm obviously the type who

19

recovers! Come on, we've forgotten to have supper, and I'm starving!'

She had to keep reminding herself, over the next few days, not to count too much on Mr Gaunt's suggestion, nor to let herself realise how much she would love to be in France again. She had never actually been to the South, but Paris had been her home from the age of ten until her grandfather died in her twentieth year. She had been in London then, and had gone back to Paris only for her grandfather's funeral, and to close up the house and see everything sold. It had seemed more practicable afterwards—and less painful—to return to London for a new life and independence. She had done several jobs since then. Her determination to be a writer hardening, she scribbled away in her spare time and sent off finished pieces which usually came back—until the success of the last few, which had encouraged her to believe she was beginning to learn. It had been, perhaps, rather a self-contained life, though Betty had become a friend since the two girls had met up through a flat-sharing advertisement; and because Sara had been an only child she was used to being solitary. She was eager to prove herself—and this chance seemed too good an opportunity to miss. But perhaps it wouldn't happen...

It did. When Mr Gaunt called her into his office, his smile showed that he had good news. More than that, he had a contract for her to sign. Glancing quickly through the document. Sara saw that it was to be a three-months trial on both sides, with an option to renew the contract monthly after that. She was a little intrigued to see that she would become an employee of Lorivel rather than of Mr Halberson himself. The difference didn't seem particularly important. Mr Gaunt asked if she wanted to take the contract away to read, but it all seemed straightforward enough so Sara shook her head, and scribbled her signature in the necessary places so that he could send the document back by the same day's post. Things were to move fast now, for she was expected at the Villa Robinet, Mr Halberson's address, in ten day's time, at the beginning of April. A flight would be booked for her from London to Nice, where she would be met and taken along the coast beyond Cannes to the area called L'Ile d'Or where the Villa Robinet was situated. 'The Island of Gold'—it was certainly a romantic address.

The travel arrangements, though, needed a little alteration. Sara asked if she might fly from Paris to Nice instead: she could take care of her own travel arrangements to Paris. It had occurred to her (though she didn't say so) that she could make her own sentimental journey, to put flowers on her grandfather's grave, something she hadn't done for some time now. It was agreed, and Sara was left in a whirl of excitement to organise her departure, sort out suitable clothes, pack, and try to leave her work and her desk tidy enough to be handed over to someone else.

Dennis had gone to Frankfurt from Amsterdam, so she didn't have to face him again. Sara was glad of that, afraid of her betraying blush if she had to see him again, unsure too that the discovery of his engagement had altered his capacity to attract her. She might have made light of it to Bet, but within herself she wasn't at all sure that she wouldn't weaken, if she had to see him. She was relieved that she was to have a couple of days to spare to finish her packing before she set out, because it meant that she would be gone from the office before he was due to return. Then, right at the end of her last day, she looked round at a sound, and saw Dennis, as fair and handsome as ever, standing smiling at her from her open office doorway.

'You're leaving us, I hear? Sara, Sara! If I hadn't come back a day early, you'd have vanished without my even seeing you!' He was giving her his best smile—designed, Bet would probably have said, to turn her knees to water, which annoyingly it did. 'I'll miss you...'

'Oh, I shall probably be back.' Her voice sounded pleasantly cool, Sara was glad to find, and she *hadn't* blushed. 'It's only for a few months—unless I manage to make my name in the meantime!' She added steadily, on a polite note, 'You'll be married, I expect, by the time I get back.'

'Needs must, my dear. The lady won't wait forever.' He didn't even look disconcerted, but continued to lounge against the doorjamb. 'I'll tell you what. You're going—when, Wednesday? That gives us a few days. We must have dinner, to say goodbye. Now let's see—not tonight, because I'm booked up. Dinner tomorrow, then?'

'No, I'm afraid I'm travelling tomorrow,' Sara heard her own voice say calmly, without a tremor. 'We'll just have to say goodbye now, won't we?' And with that she smiled at him, picked up her bag, and walked past him. It was a triumph that she had sounded so casual. She heard him say behind her, 'Oh—well—enjoy yourself, then!' and this time he did sound a little disconcerted, even faintly injured.

Well, she had resisted him, anyway. Walking smoothly so it did not look like flight, Sara took refuge in the Ladies, and peered at herself in the mirror. She was glad to see that she still wasn't blushing. No, he wouldn't make a fool of her again! But oh, to be tall and smoothly sophisticated, instead of her petite self with long fair hair inclined towards an unruly curl if allowed, and piled now on top of her head in a loose coronet. More than anything, she would have liked to look cool, elegant and capable. Frowning a little, she decided to brush her hair hard and coil it into a bun while she was in France. Perhaps horn-rimmed glasses might help? Not that she needed them, but they might improve her image.

She had told Dennis a lie about her travelling date: well, she would fulfil that lie and go tomorrow. She had no friends in Paris nowadays, but she could wander round for a couple of days revisiting old haunts, with her plane ticket for Thursday morning in her handbag. This early in the season, it would be quite easy to get a place on the cross-channel ferry without booking, and she could easily enough find a *pension* to stay at. Now, it was certainly time she stopped hiding in here, and went to say her goodbyes.

Bet insisted on seeing her off next day. She seemed, at this last minute, far more anxious about everything than Sara was. 'Mother-hen!' Sara teased as she leaned out of the train window to speak to her friend on the platform. 'I don't know what you think is going to happen to me—but I *have* been looking after myself for years, you know!'

'All the same, be careful, won't you?'

'What, with the old man? I don't think he's going to be dangerous! If I meet any other wolves I'll run away at once, I promise!' Sara gave her an impish grin, too excited for the memory of Dennis to spoil her happiness. She was off, on her way to the South of France, and nothing could possibly go wrong with a perfectly simple and well-planned journey.

Two days later she remembered her own confidence ruefully. There was an air traffic controller's strike, all over France. No, *mam'selle,* sorry, there will be no flights from Paris to Nice for the rest of the week at least. A Gallic shrug accompanied the information. If her journey was urgent, there was always the train.

There was the train, it seemed, or nothing; the train which hurtled across France through the night, leaving Paris at eleven. Sara sent a careful telegram to the Villa Robinet, trying to make it sound as efficient as possible. 'WILL MAKE MY OWN WAY TO VILLA. ARRIVING FRIDAY. SARA FARROW.'

was her final version. A thoughtful study of the map showed her that, to get to the Ile d'Or region, she would do better to get off the train at St Raphael then to go on to Nice. She was sure she could find some transport to take her on from there, since the nearest village to the Villa Robinet was Boulouris, and that was shown to be quite close to St Raphael along the coast. St Raphael would be a ten-hour journey, and it seemed a shame to Sara to be crossing the whole of France in the dark without seeing it, but she had no choice. With her place on the train booked, she went back to the *pension* she had only just left and persuaded Madame to give her her room back for the day, so that she could rest and change. Her luggage was easy; one medium-sized suitcase had been all air travel would allow, so she only had that and her portable typewriter. She had already concluded that she would have to buy more clothes in France if necessary.

French trains were always particularly French: there was something formal and correct about them. Edging round a large family party saying goodbye with everybody kissing everybody in turn on both cheeks. Sara tried to suppress a yawn as she made her way along the platform, and changed her heavy suitcase from one hand to the other. She hadn't managed to sleep during her afternoon's wait, and, oh dear, it would be difficult to look capable and alert when she met Mr Halberson if she didn't get much sleep all night either. There were *couchettes* (the six-berth sleeping compartments) on this train, but they were all booked up: her seat was in an ordinary carriage. At the moment she looked like any student, since that had seemed the best way to travel—jeans, shirt, jumper, and an anorak: she could always shed a layer if the weather grew warmer further south, though it certainly wasn't warm here and now, with a chilly wind whipping round her ankles. She had even braided her hair as the best way to keep it tidy, and had left it hanging down her back in a childish pigtail. As she plodded along the length of the long train, with its high steps up to the carriages, Sara caught sight of a steward in his round peaked cap and shiny-buttoned uniform, consulting a list in his hand while he talked to someone. She hesitated: was it worth asking if there was a *couchette* free after all, and offering to pay the extra charge? Eleven o'clock at night suddenly seemed very late, and she was tired...

She stepped closer, but as she paused, the man talking to the steward finished his conversation abruptly and swung round. He was tall—surprisingly tall for a Frenchman, though he certainly *looked* French—and his movement brought him straight into Sara's path, so that he almost tripped over her. She murmured a quick, *'Pardon, monsieur,'* though it had hardly been her fault; and then regretted her politeness when he looked through her rather than at her. He stepped round her impatiently as if she had been an insect. She heard him give an exasperated murmur under his breath which was no more irritated than *she* felt considering he had made her drop her typewriter on her foot. She made to glare after him as he walked away—but something, tiredness perhaps, made her stare instead with a startled catch in her throat. He really was amazingly handsome. She had seen as much as she looked up into his face, and into a pair of dark eyes which had seemed to bore right through her and out the other side. At least, she amended quickly, he *would* be amazingly handsome if he hadn't looked so bad-tempered. Almost as beautiful as her Rumanian violinist of long ago. Well-dressed too; his formal dark suit had fitted him to perfection.

Sara shook herself, and looked round for the steward, but he had vanished back into the train. Serve her right for gazing gooey-eyed after someone who was undoubtedly one of Bet's wolves; and wouldn't Bet have scolded her? Sara gave a weak little giggle at her own foolishness. Well, she *was* tired; and the last few days had held a lot of mixed emotions. Not least, the emotion of being back in her beloved France, and visiting her grandfather's grave, with it's plain inscription, 'Carl Farrow—Musician.' He had wanted it as simple as that, however famous he had been as a conductor. There were no graves to visit for her parents, because the aeroplane in which they had been travelling had crashed into deep water and remained there. Her father's only memorial lay in recordings of the music he had played so beautifully on the oboe, before his career had been tragically cut short. And her mother's? Well, her mother's memorial lay in being Justin Farrow's wife—and loving him enough to give up her own career as a pianist to go with him wherever he went.

Yes, there *had* been too many emotions in the past few days, Sara decided, feeling a childish sting of tears behind her eyes for old tragedies as she finally found her compartment and heaved her luggage into it, stowing it neatly beneath the upright seats. A young couple were already dozing in one corner. This part of the train was scarcely full. Sara sank gratefully into an opposite corner seat, and leaned back against the high head-rest. It had been lovely to wander round Paris again. She had felt almost tempted to stay in Paris and find a job there—French, particularly Parisian French, was second-nature to her, and she could type, or work in a shop—anything. But no; she wanted to be a writer, didn't she? To use the skills she had been working so hard to learn, and use them well? So she must accept challenges. And—a certain amount of loneliness? Confused, more than a little depressed, she huddled down in her seat, wishing she had remembered to bring something with her to eat. She had an apple somewhere in her bag, if she could be bothered to get it out. She closed her eyes for a moment, and heard whistles blowing a few minutes later, then felt a jerk as the train started its journey. It seemed easier to keep her eyes closed: there would be nothing much to see.

★ ★ ★ ★

She didn't know how long she had slept when she came awake with a start, wondering where she was and why her neck was stiff. She was muddled, too, by her dreams: Dennis had been somewhere in them, and her grandfather, and Darjan Aram the Rumanian, looking just as he had in the old days. He was staring at her. She came awake properly to find that someone *was* staring at her, but it wasn't Darjan—even if she fancied for a confused moment that it was him, and even began a tentative smile. But it was someone else, watching her intently from the seat opposite out of very dark eyes. Sara gulped as she recognised the man from the station platform; the one who had tripped over her, and looked so cross about it. He didn't look any less cross now: he was gazing at her with a kind of moody intentness, and he certainly didn't attempt to answer the half-smile she had unintentionally given him.

He seemed suddenly to realise that she was gazing back at him, and averted his eyes quickly. Perhaps, after all, he hadn't meant to stare; she had just been in his eyeline. Sara pulled herself together, and glanced cautiously around to make sure that the young couple were still in the carriage too: she wasn't sure that she wanted to be alone in the compartment with this stranger. They were reassuringly present, even if asleep. She automatically smoothed her hair in its unaccustomed pigtail, and tried to settle back into her corner. A look at her watch showed that it was almost one o'clock, still early by the night's reckoning, so she hadn't really slept all that long. It was a pity she hadn't brought anything with her to read. She glanced under her lashes at the man opposite her, and saw that he was still sitting with his face averted, gazing towards the darkened window.

Since he was still looking away, she could study him covertly. In fact it was difficult *not* to stare, because he really was extraordinarily handsome, with the very dark, classical good looks which Frenchmen sometimes have, combined with a length of limb unusual in that small-statured race. His hair was almost blue-black, his eyes a heavy-lidded dark brown, while his chin had an almost alarming firmness. A straight nose, a fainly olive-tinted skin which was smooth without losing masculinity.

It was a pity, Sara thought, that his mouth had a slightly cynical twist, which must be his natural expression if he adopted it even when staring into space, as now. He looked out of place in this ordinary railway carriage, because everything about him suggested wealth, though discreetly—his suit; his cream shirt which must be silk as was his tie, in a heavier weight; his highly-polished shoes. He wore a small gold signet ring on the little finger of his right hand, and the wafer-slim watch on his opposite wrist was gold too. He should be travelling in a private jet instead of a common-or-garden train. Sara found herself thinking, with complete idiocy, that if she had to run into someone who looked like that, it was unfair that she couldn't have been looking her best, instead of her scruffiest. A small smile curved her lips at her own foolishness, and she looked down quickly, hoping he hadn't been able to feel her gazing at him. Though probably, looking like that, he was used to it!

She glanced idly towards the window—and caught his eyes watching her in the darkened glass. She felt a blush starting; this was ridiculous! But at that moment the carriage door was pulled back with a crash, and a uniformed steward appeared, bracing himself against the sway of the train. He spoke directly and with deference to the dark man, ignoring Sara. There was a vacant *couchette* after all, *m'sieur,* a cancelled booking. If *m'sieur* would care to follow him? The carriage door crashed again and the two men were gone, before Sara could pull herself together enough to catch the steward's attention and ask him if there were any more cancelled *couchettes*. Oh well, it didn't matter, after all, as there was room now to stretch out along the seat here—but she couldn't help feeling that noticeable wealth obviously carried advantages.

The rest of the journey was long, but without incident. Sara dozed, half-sleeping, half-waking, conscious of the pounding of wheels beneath her, soothing her. She came awake at Toulon to footsteps and voices and a sky still dark; on again then until the stop at Marseilles woke her properly to daylight. And warmth. Leaning from the train window and wishing she could stop to explore France's second city with all its romantic and dangerous associations, Sara felt the soft warmth of the southern air on her skin. A trolley on the platform was selling hot chocolate and croissants or brioches to the wakening travellers, and Sara nipped out to buy herself some, dunking her croissant as the French did and enjoying the warm, dripping pastry. When the train started again she went to splash her face and hands with cold water in the tiny washroom, then sat watching, fascinated, as grey-green fields and huddles of farm buildings unrolled themselves past the window, with rows of cypresses and olive-trees lending a darker green and silver-grey. Here, away from the industrial cities, it was possible to realise how much of France was still an agricultural country run on a peasant economy.

Excitement was beginning to rise in her again, to go with the pounding of the train's wheels. This was the south—Mediterranean country—the country of Languedoc, and passionate legends; of Van Gogh with his mad, hot paintings; of burning sun and flaring temperament, more Italianate in its emotions than her own staid north. And on the coast there would be mimosa, and palm-trees, and the blue sparkling sea.

The young couple were awake and exchanged smiles with Sara, then conversation. They were going on to Nice, but they knew St Raphael well enough to be able to tell her that she could take a bus along the coast road to Boulouris from right outside St Raphael station. They obviously took her for a student like themselves, since they didn't suggest she could afford a taxi (though a taxi-rank was mentioned near the bus terminal). Then the train shot through Fréjus—the one broken golden stone column all that could be seen of its famous Roman Amphitheatre, and then they were slowing down to pull into St Raphael station. Sara said her goodbyes, exchanged good-luck wishes, and jumped down on to the platform with the boy student helpfully passing her luggage down to her. Well, she had got this far: now, she thought briskly, she would find a Ladies and change herself into the efficient-looking Miss Farrow whom old Mr Halberson would be expecting. He could scarcely blame her for being a day late, in the circumstances. Still, she resisted the temptation to stare round her at St Raphael's rather featureless railway station, or to loiter enjoying the warm breeze which smelled of the sea somewhere out of sight. Instead she made straight for the platform exit with determination in her step.

It was only half-past nine in the morning, so she felt able to take her time. In the very clean Ladies Room on the station forecourt a dragon-like lady in an overall made sure she paid her two francs for a wash and brush up. The woman scowled when she saw Sara open her suitcase, but withdrew to her cubicle with a sniff. Sara changed quickly into a navy pleated skirt, bought for its uncrushable properties, and a crisp white cotton blouse with long sleeves: then she unplaited her hair, brushed it into shining smoothness, and coiled it into a tight and tidy bun on her neck. Very little make-up, though just enough to avoid a clean-scrubbed schoolgirl look; and a pair of smoky-lensed glasses which gave her, she thought, a serious air, but could double as sunglasses. (And the sun *was* shining, too, which was a blissful change after London.) High sling-backed sandals gave her extra height, instead of the flat pumps she had travelled in. A careful scrutiny told her that she would do. Now to make enquiries to find out where, around Boulouris, the Villa Robinet might be, and to see if a taxi would take her there.

The taxi-rank, full earlier, had abruptly emptied while she changed. However, a Tour

Agency which also hired out cars was open, just across the wide street which instead of palm-trees had limes along the middle of it; and Sara decided to go there in search of information. She pushed open the glass door, finding the interior shadowy after the brightness of the street, and crossed quickly to one end of the counter where she could see a clerk was free. He was immersed in a list in front of him, so she raised her voice a little to get his attention.

'Excuse me, *m'sieur*—would you happen to know how I can reach the Villa Robinet, near Boulouris? Or *at* Boulouris—I'm not sure which—'

'You are looking for the Villa Robinet?' A deep voice spoke nearby—in French, as she had done—with a note of enquiry. 'Are you by any chance Miss Sara Farrow?'

Turning, Sara began, 'Yes, I am—' And then stopped dead. As large as life, moving towards her from where he must have been standing further along the counter, was the man from the train. 'Yes, I—I am,' she stammered again; and then blurted out, 'Who are *you*?'

The merest lift of an eyebrow was his only acknowledgement of the rudeness in her voice. 'I am Paul Merinard,' he said coolly, standing over her, as darkly handsome as ever. Sara only came up to his shoulder and had to tilt her head to look up at him, which somehow put her even more at a disadvantage. While she stood trying to gather her scattered wits he went on, switching to English, a sarcastic note coming into his voice. 'Paul Merinard, Miss Farrow. You must know the name, since you signed a contract of employment with me little more than a week ago! And I have wasted a great deal of time trying to contact you for the past two days!'

'You—you've been trying to contact me?' Sara asked, confused. Was *that* why he had stared at her on the train? If so, why hadn't he said anything?

'Must you repeat what I say? If you'd kept to the travel arrangements I gave you, it would have saved us both a lot of trouble! However—'

He broke off, a swift frown drawing his brows together. Sara, who had pushed her dark glasses up on to her head so as to see him better, saw a startled recognition come into his eyes. He gave her a swift, raking glance from head to foot; and there was a quality in the look which sparked her anger. Abruptly, and on a note of disbelief, he said, '*You* are Sara Farrow?'

'Is there any reason why I shouldn't be?' Attack was the best method of defence, so Sara went on quickly, haughtily. 'I'm sorry if you've been looking for me, but there was an air traffic controllers' strike—as I'm sure you know! However, I did send a telegram! I hope Mr Halberson wasn't worried—'

'My great-uncle, unfortunately, is dead. And if you hadn't gone jaunting off to Paris—to see a boyfriend?—you would have known about it, and saved yourself a journey!'

'He's—he's *dead*?'

'It was very sudden: a heart attack.' He was still speaking English, impeccably. 'At his age, I suppose one could expect no less. Since you didn't even know my great-uncle, surely you're not going to burst into tears?'

Sara gasped at the unfairness of the sarcasm in his tone, and glared at him as she struggled with her feelings. Abruptly he seemed to make up his mind, and slid a hand under her elbow.

'Come.'

'Come? Come where?'

'I have a hired car which should be outside by now. We may as well make the rest of the journey together.' A slight stress on "the rest" seemed somehow sinister, and it seemed unnecessary that he should hold her arm, so that Sara tried to pull away from him. His fingers tightened—and his touch, confusingly, seemed to send a current of electricity through her. 'I might have felt inclined to send you back on the next train,' he said smoothly, 'if I'd managed to catch up with you in Paris, but since you've come this far, that would hardly be fair. Besides—' there was a silkily ironic note in his voice—'you look so presentable, and you're obviously taking so much trouble, that I think I must find you something to do to repay your efforts. We can talk about it as we drive.'

Sara found herself walking meekly towards the door. If he *was* Paul Merinard—and presumably he was—she supposed he felt responsible for her. The Merinards owned Lorivel, and she had arrived to be a Lorivel employee, however pointless that had now become. Dazed with disappointment, she climbed into the front of the hired Citroen when he opened the door for her, and allowed him to stow her suitcase and typewriter in the back with his own grip. He got in himself, started the car, and they moved smoothly out into the morning traffic.

Sara knew that she should be thinking of something sensible to say. As the boulevard opened out, with luxury shops each side of it, she caught a glimpse ahead of a forest of masts, then a flash of sea beyond the harbour, looking incredibly blue in the sunlight. It all seemed unreal. All she was really conscious of was the broad, dark-clad shoulder so close to her, and a pair of strong olive-skinned hands on the wheel. Which of the Merinards was he, she wondered? He looked in his early thirties. She must stop feeling daunted by his sarcastic manner, and ask him some reasonable questions.

'If you'd guessed who I was on the train, why didn't you say so?' she blurted out.

44

'I didn't. I merely thought, innocence is out of style.' Before she could do more than take in the words, he went on, with a cynical note in his voice which appalled her, 'And then you woke up, and I knew that I was right, of course! The twenty-year-old innocent turned into a little sophisticate who tried to give me the eye the moment she was conscious. It was—amusing—to watch you working out the best way to start a conversation with me. So tell me, Miss Sara Farrow—if we hadn't been interrupted, how would you have set about making the pick-up? We're alone now, and you have my undivided attention!'

CHAPTER TWO

Sara felt as if her breath had been shocked out of her body: it was his tone rather than his words which had made the question insulting, but the conceit of it made her stare at him with her mouth half open and a sweeping tide of anger bringing scarlet to her cheeks. There was no reason at all why she shouldn't have chatted to him on the train save for her own instinctive shyness, and the formality which her grandfather's housekeeper, with typical French middle-class propriety, had instilled into her as a child—which always, somehow, came back to her when she was in France—but the manner in which he said 'pick-up' made his meaning obvious and left her seething. She remembered, with horror, that she *had* studied him on the train and thought how handsome he was, and had felt curious about him; she remembered too that he had caught her studying him. Her silence now seemed to amuse him, and when she heard him give a low chuckle, she finally found her voice.

'Perhaps you would be kind enough to take me back to the station, Monsieur Merinard! I'm sure you can explain to—to whoever runs your firm, that I decided in the circumstances to go back to Paris and look for work there!'

'Ah, so there *is* a boyfriend in Paris! Last night you were merely thinking of spreading your favours around a bit?'

'Certainly not in *your* direction, *monsieur*,' Sara retorted tartly. She had switched to French, because the formality of the language seemed to lend her dignity, and her impulsive decision that she didn't want to spend any more time in this man's company seemed to lend her steadiness. 'I'm sure there's no way of convincing you of that fact when you're determined to jump to conclusions, so please will you stop the car and let me get out?' She realised as she spoke that he was increasing speed rather than slowing down, and going further away from the station with every second: they were travelling along a wide esplanade now with the sea on one side, large hotels and a Casino on the other, the holiday area of the town spreading out around them. 'Please stop the car!' Sara repeated more sharply.

'No, I'm certainly not going to dump you at the roadside. And there's no point in your play-acting chagrin by leaping out at the first traffic lights we came to, either, you'd merely lose your luggage. Thank you for demonstrating the excellence of your French. As your employer, I'm glad to know that your qualifications are as stated. Yes, *I* run Lorivel, as you should know if you read your contract properly!' He paused, but not long enough for Sara to answer him. 'Now that we've established that I can see through you, so it won't be worth your trying out any of your tricks on me, we can establish a proper working relationship, I think. So, Miss Farrow—'

'But surely *you're* not—' Sara broke off: she had been going to say that he was too young to be the head of Lorival, family firm or no, but there seemed no point in following that up. The job she had come out to do no longer existed so she wouldn't have to work for *any* of the Merinard family. 'There's no need for us to have a working relationship,' she said with as much dignity as she could muster. 'Since Mr Halberson's dead, of course I shall go back straight away...'

Her voice tailed off, because disappointment was hitting her again. The job had seemed so promising—and besides, her eye couldn't help being drawn to the dancing blue of the Mediterranean on their right as they swept out of the outskirts of the town. Bluey-green pines began to edge the road with the sea glimpsed in snatches between them. Villas, snug amongst the pines, caught the sunlight on pink-washed walls and terracotta-tiled roofs behind tall railings which protected the lush greenery of gardens and the ever-present sea beyond. There was a brightness in the air, a southern dryness, a promise of heat to come, and where the road curved to follow the coast, a gap in the pines showed craggy red rocks edging the arc of a white-sanded beach.

'Yes, it's beautiful, isn't it?' Paul Merinard

answered her thought. 'The Esterel coast is one of the loveliest in France—particularly now, before it gets too crowded. And since the tourist season hasn't fully begun yet, so that it *isn't* too crowded, there shouldn't be too much to distract you from work! Yes, I think there'll be plenty to do to keep you out of mischief. You can sort through my great-uncle's papers. There's an enormous number of them, and they'll have to be put in some sort of order.'

'No, thank you. I came here to be a writer, not a filing clerk!'

'You're not in a position to say no thank you, Miss Farrow. We have a contract—which I must say you *don't* seem to have read!—making you a Lorivel employee for the next three months. Renewable,' Paul Merinard added coolly, keeping his eyes on the road and not bothering to look round at Sara's outraged face. 'The contract doesn't specify *what* you are to do, so I could put you on to housework if I chose! Not that I shall: I don't suppose you're very good at it. It seems perfectly fair to me, since sorting through my great-uncle's papers would have been part of your job in any case, to ask you to do it—so if I *were* to sue you for breach of contract, I'm sure I'd win!'

'You wouldn't—' Sara began disbelievingly, but he overrode her.

'Why not? I've brought you out here in good faith, and paid your expenses. Any court would merely think you were being unreasonable!'

That was probably true, however much her dislike of his high-handed behaviour towards her made her want to fight him. Sara bit her lip. She *didn't* want to work for him...but she did want to stay in France. And the glimpse she had had so far of this lovely Provencal region with its warm, wild beauty and strange sense of joy in the air was tugging at her imagination, making her want to explore all its contrasts. She stole another glance at Paul Merinard's profile, stubbornness warring with good sense. The only way to deal with him was to try to keep her composure—but how much would she have to see of this unbelievably handsome man, if, as he said, he was her direct employer? She asked, hesitantly.

'Who would I actually be working for?'

'Lorivel. In effect, me. Why—were you thinking that there might be someone higher up to whom you could appeal? I'm sorry to disappoint you, but there isn't some older man you could approach with quivering lip—' his lips curved in cynical amusement at her tiny, suppressed choke—'because since my father's death five years ago, I *am* head of the firm. It was me with whom you exchanged signatures on that binding contract—and I assure you, I *do* intend to make use of you!'

'As a—a filing clerk?'

'What else had you in mind?'

'Writing the history of Lorivel!' Sara said very rapidly, aware that her cheeks were scarlet again (if they had ever stopped being) but aware too, that the smooth undertone of mockery in his voice had a disturbing effect on her. She rushed on quickly, trying to sound as coolly efficient as possible, 'Presumably you still want that done, Monsieur Merinard, and if all the papers are there—'

'Yes, I suppose I might still commission it some time. You're nothing if not ambitious, it seems. I must say—' he frowned—'when my godfather recommended you, I wasn't expecting someone so...young. What have you been doing so far—working as a secretary?'

'No, as an editor! And I've had several things published—which I'm sure you must know, because I'm certain Mr Gaunt must have told your—your godfather when he suggested me! Mr Gaunt,' Sara added stiffly, 'is—was—my employer, at Gaunt Press, in London—'

'Yes, I know Matthew Gaunt, and he *is* my godfather. He's a distant relative of my mother's—who was English, so you don't need to go on proving your capabilities by talking to me in French. I hope,' Paul Merinard said moodily, and with unnecessary rudeness, Sara felt, 'that Matthew didn't send you to me because he wanted to get rid of you—but I suppose I can trust him further than that! I shall expect you to work hard, Miss Farrow, and not cause any trouble—I hope you understand that!'

Sara opened her mouth, shut it again, and tried not to feel shaken all over again. Mr Gaunt hadn't mentioned his connection with

53

the Merinards; and *had* he sent her out here to get rid of her? Not for the reasons Paul Merinard might assume, that her work was unsatisfactory, but out of kindness? She moistened suddenly dry lips, but her suspicions, which might have dispirited her, strengthened her resolve. She would prove herself to be so efficient that even Paul Merinard would have to take back his odious assumptions about her—just let him see if she wouldn't! She found her voice, and said coldly, 'Very well, Monsieur Merinard. I accept the contract of work I signed with you. And if you really haven't had the sense to check on my references before you decided to employ me, I suggest you write to Mr Gaunt again and ask him just what work I *have* been doing! I think you'll find that it's been perfectly satisfactory!'

If she had hoped to dent his complacency a little, it didn't look as if she had succeeded: he merely raised an eyebrow as he drew up smoothly at a set of traffic lights to let an old woman with a basket cross the road. Sara, taking a swift look round, saw that this must be

Boulouris—or one edge of it at least—since a corner café bore the name and so did a large supermarket, though the village didn't extend to both sides of the main road but had merely the same pine trees and the entrance to a park on its coastal side. The road they were on must, she supposed, be part of the Corniche d'Or, the coastal highway which wound round next to the sea all the way from St Raphael through to Cannes. As they started off again she saw that large holiday complexes were appearing now amongst the trees to their left—all sorts of trees, pines, a few palms, and large trees with grey-green bushy tops and twisted silvery trunks which stretched away up the hill where the ground rose into steep terraces on the landward side. Here and there a sliced section of the red rock showed how the road had been carved out of the rising ground. And on the right, increasingly, there were gaps in the trees where small bays had fretted into the land, each with its smooth white arc of beach, and the warm rough redness of the rocks stretching arms out into the dancing, sparkling blue of the sea.

Here and there the white sails of small boats curved their elegant shapes against the water, and Sara caught sight of a bright red triangle held up by the balance of a windsurfer. Even this early in the day, holiday-makers were taking advantage of the sun and light wind which blew in off the sea. Craning round to see whether the windsurfer would right himself from a near-tumble Sara felt the excitement of being here begin to bubble up in her again in spite of everything. She was conscious of a sharp rising curve in the road, and then Paul Merinard swung right abruptly and stopped, hooting a sharp blast on his horn.

They were facing dark, heavy railings between stone columns, as firmly closed as a prison gate—and with something of the same menacing air, lent perhaps by the neglected look of the trees and bushes which crowded thickly against the edges of a gravelled drive. The drive bent sharply so that there was no sign of the house beyond, except, high up amongst the still-crowding trees, the glimpse of one grey stone corner and the dark pointed edge of a roof. Paul hooted again, impatiently;

and as an old man shuffled out from the bushes beside the drive to peer at them, then began pulling at the gates, Sara saw the faded sign carved on one of the stone columns—Villa Robinet. It all looked so much less promising than any of the other villas they had passed, with their bright pastel colours and hump-tiled red or green roofs and well-kept, if lush- gardens, that Sara gave an involuntary little shiver. It was almost as if the sun had gone in...

'My great-uncle was something of a recluse,' Paul Merinard said coolly. He made a sign of thanks to the old gardener as the car moved forward with a crunch onto the gravelled drive. 'Since he never married but lived alone, he retreated more and more into his memories as he grew older. Marie, the housekeeper, is growing old too, we'll have to pension her off once the villa is cleared. Your job—Miss Farrow—will be to try to separate his personal papers from the ones concerning the firm, and set the whole lot into some kind of date order. I think you may find it a mammoth task.'

He didn't have to sound as if setting her a mammoth task pleased him so much, Sara thought resentfully; but she was peering ahead to try to see what the Villa Robinet itself was like. The trees came up so close to the house that it was difficult to get more than an impression of a large grey shape which might have had elegant lines if more space had been cleared around it, and if it had been painted instead of left to a grey stone shabbiness. It was a tall house, for sure, but badly darkened by the growth all around it; and although it must stand above the sea, there was no view because the gardens had been left to run wild, leaving no more than a frustrating feeling that the sea must be there somewhere beyond the thickness of the trees. There were pines again, heavy and dark, with some of the grey-green bushy-topped trees in amongst them, but with no sign of the bright-flowered mimosa Sara had hoped to see—in fact, now she thought about it, there had been no more than the occasional dusty bunch of dying yellow all along the coast road. It must come and go early in this part of the south, she thought with disappointment; though since this was only April, perhaps there was a second flowering.

She was trying not to feel daunted by the dark neglect of the Villa Robinet when Paul Merinard drew up abruptly outside a heavy front door, and switched off the engine. He turned and gave Sara an assessing look, as if he could feel her doubts, and that made her stiffen her spine and try to blank her face into a polite look of interest. She was also wondering, with a sudden wariness, whether Paul Merinard was to be in residence at the Villa Robinet too.

'Marie should have a room ready for you, since I sent her a message to that effect. Come,' Paul Merinard said briefly.

'Is—is there a telephone here?' Sara asked. Somehow, imagination suggested that she would feel like the princess in the tower if there wasn't even that.

'Yes, there is—though Marie dislikes using it, as she's rather deaf, so she frequently doesn't answer. However, I *shan't* expect to find that you've been making long gossipy calls across the length of France—nor to England, for that matter!' he told her with a note of caustic warning in his voice. Once again, he didn't give her a chance to answer, or to point out that she wasn't the irresponsible teenager he seemed to take her for: instead he got out of the car, leaving her wordless and resentful. It was more than a pity, Sara thought with anger, that he had seen her first in her travelling clothes and formed his own arbitrary judgement of her. She pulled crossly at the door handle and swung the door wide, just as he came round the car with the apparent intention of opening it for her.

Good manners was certainly something she wouldn't have expected from him. Sara gave him what she hoped was a dignified look, and swung her legs out of the car. As she stood up, she found her dignity going for nothing, since she had forgotten the gravel and one high-heeled sandal turned over abruptly on it, sending her stumbling. What was worse, it sent her stumbling straight into the tall dark figure which stood there waiting for her. One dark-clad arm caught her firmly and steadied her: for the space of a heart-beat she was aware that she was clinging to him, held firmly against his chest. She caught her breath in a gasp, feeling the swift, electrical tremor of his closeness. Then she was set firmly back on her feet, with a space between them, and Paul Merinard was drawling with that odious cynicism.

'That, Miss Farrow, is the oldest trick in the book! Didn't I warn you that I'd seen them all? Oh, and by the way—if you were thinking of going in for that English fashion of claiming "sexual harassment", first of all I don't think it's taken seriously in France, and secondly, in the circumstances, don't you think anyone might question *who* is harassing *whom*?'

He turned away with no more than an amused glance for her angry expression and scarlet cheeks, leaving her to follow him to the front door. Sara—left again with nothing to say—cast his back view a look of anger and intense dislike which was totally wasted because he didn't even bother to glance round. He was an expert at making something out of nothing, she told herself furiously, as she picked her way across the gravel carefully after him with a reminding ache in her slightly-wrenched ankle. He was quite the most appalling, cynical man she had ever met...but she had to acknowledge that the rapid tattoo her heart was beating was not just from anger. For that brief second when he had held her against him, she had felt a startling awareness of his attraction, so dizzying in its intensity that it had taken her breath away; and, confusingly, she had felt an awareness from him, too. But as for the suggestion that she had fallen against him on purpose, that really was too much....!

She reached him in silence just as the heavy front door opened, giving her somewhere to look instead of having to take care to keep her eyes cast down lest he should read anything besides anger in them. She knew, bitterly, that he would only think she was angry because he had seen through her; and she wondered again how on earth she was going to manage to work for him. Trying to concentrate, and keeping her head held high, she realised that she was staring too hard at the old woman who opened the door to them. And, for one short moment, the old woman had stared at her,

too—with a look of such extraordinary malevolence that Sara almost flinched.

No, she must have imagined it; for the old
woman was speaking to Paul Merinard now
with nothing more than the slightly blank
expression of the elderly. She was saying, in
a thick accent which Sara had to strain to
disentangle from its unusual vowel-sounds and
stressed consonants, that she had received
Monsieur's message and made everything
ready, so they had better come in—and if there
was a slightly resentful note in her voice, it
was no more than the normal complaint of an
old servant. She was dressed in the standard
rusty black of the widow and her face was
seamed into an incredible network of lines, so
that it would be hard to know how old she
actually was behind that lined and weather-
beaten skin; but she was no taller than Sara
herself, and could hardly be said to be a
frightening figure with her bent shoulders and
straggly grey hair. In fact, Sara realised with
a sudden rush of sympathy, the old woman's
eyes were reddened a little as if from weep-
ing, and she had, after all, lost an employer

of whom she might have been fond only two days ago.

She found that she was being introduced to Marie, and shook hands with the French correctness: then they were going inside, into a dark, gloomy, brown painted hall, which had, nevertheless, obviously been polished with great care since no speck of dust was visible in its gloomy interior. A flight of stairs wound up to a higher storey with a window letting in a shaft of greenish sunlight through the leaves. The place was bare and carpetless and surrounded by dark-painted closed doors. With the front door now closed behind them, it was rather like being in an underground cave, Sara thought with a sudden flight of fancy, and it was as cold as a cave too, with a slightly musty smell in the air in spite of all the polish. She wanted to shiver, and had to restrain her instinct to move closer to Paul Merinard—reminding herself bitterly that she knew only too well what he would make of that!

Old Marie was saying something in a grumbling voice about the place not really being suitable for a young person; however, if Monsieur insisted, she would do her best. And was the young person really to be allowed into Mr Halberson's study, which he had not even liked Marie to clean or dust? While Paul Merinard was answering her, firmly if soothingly, Sara was almost sure she caught a flash of that same malevolence in Marie's sidelong glance in her direction. If she resented her arrival, with old Mr Halberson so recently dead, that was perhaps understandable—but even so Sara had that shivery feeling again. The house seemed to have its own looming presence, heavy with age and long-dead disappointments, so that it oppressed her and made her glance round the bare hallway uncertainly; it almost felt as if the old man were still lying in state, dead upstairs...Sara hoped with swift horror that his body *wasn't* still upstairs, then pulled herself together rapidly with the knowledge that she was being ridiculous. When Paul Merinard turned to her and started speaking in English she jumped guiltily and made herself listen to him.

'I don't know whether you can follow Marie's accent—though no doubt you'll communicate well enough when you get used to it. I'll leave you now. Marie will show you round, and tell you where everything is. She'll provide your meals—but please be considerate and eat at the times she's used to, and if you want something changed, ask her politely! She's an old servant and set in her ways. I presume you're responsible enough to organise your own working hours, but I *shall* expect the work to be done!'

'Are—are *you* staying here?'

'No. There'll only be yourself and Marie sleeping in the house.' She was aware that the cynical look had come back into his eyes as he looked down at her; but it was nervousness which had prompted her question. 'I *live* somewhere else; near Grasse, in fact. Any more questions, Miss Farrow?'

'How—how can I get hold of you? If there are any questions I need to ask?' Sara added hastily. For this moment, she didn't care what he made of her unwillingness to let him go without telling her how to contact him: the oppression of the house, and her feeling of hostility from the old woman, made even *his* odious presence seem preferable to being left alone here.

'I'll leave you my office telephone number. My secretary can always take a message,' Paul Merinard said repressively—just as if Sara had *actually* been clinging to his arm, instead of just wishing she could. 'Right, that's all, then! Shall I wish you a pleasant stay in the South of France? Or just a hard-working one?'

'Of course I shall work hard, monsieur,' Sara said coldly. At least his scornful view of her had a stiffening effect on her nerves. She hesitated, then went on, as coolly, 'Will it be possible for me to have a key to the house, so that I can come in and go out as I please?'

'Hm. Yes, I suppose so.' He gave her a judging, thoughtful look, and then turned to Marie. After a moment's conversation (which seemed to contain some protest from the old woman which Sara could only partially follow) he turned back to Sara again; and back to English. 'You *may* have a key, but Marie bolts the doors at night, so don't imagine you can come in and out at all hours. Also, you may *not* invite people in here—it's private property!'

'I wasn't intending to! And how could I, anyway, when I don't know anybody?' Even as she asked the question, Sara knew with sinking heart what sort of answer he was going to make of that: as if he could see her knowledge in her eyes, he merely gave her a look and didn't bother to make the comment. She gave him an angry glance—but as he was now obviously gathering himself to depart, she made haste to put another request.

'Please would you tell Marie exactly where I am allowed to go? Which rooms I'm to use? She might very well resent my being here.' He obviously thought she was fussing and this was reflected by the boredom in his eyes. 'It would be quite understandable if she did, and I'd like to have everything quite clear, please!' protested Sara.

He turned back to the old woman, instructing her that Sara was to be allowed to go anywhere she pleased, and go through any desk or box of papers she found. Marie listened in silence and in apparent compliance. Then, at last, and with a further bored look in Sara's direction, he did prepare to leave. She had to stop him again.

'The telephone number, monsieur? There *may* be things I want to ask about Lorivel—papers I'm not sure about!'

He drew a card from his pocket, scribbled something on it with a gold pen, and handed it to her, impatience oozing through every pore. It had been a reasonable request, Sara thought angrily, and he *didn't* have to look at her as if it wasn't! 'Thank you,' she said coldly. 'I'll try not to bother your *secretary* unnecessarily. Oh—Monsieur Merinard?'

'Yes, what now?' He was at the door.

'While we *are* getting things quite clear—could you please try to realise that I'm not straight out of school, I'm a twenty-four-year-old career girl? And furthermore,' Sara added, with as much dignity as she could muster, 'if you treat *all* your employees so rudely, I'm surprised *any* of them stay with you!'

'Really? Perhaps I have them all tied to unbreakable contracts—Miss Farrow.'

She might have known that he wouldn't let her get the last word; but at least, as the door closed behind him, she had the satisfaction of knowing that, just for once, she had managed to say what she wanted to say to him. Not that it would make any difference to his arrogance, she was sure; and she was aware that looking at him had made her tremble at the knees even while she spoke. There was something about his supercilious good looks which had a disastrous effect on her, but at least he had gone now, and without her losing any more of her dignity. She could start her job properly, and without his overbearing presence.

She glanced round quickly, to find old Marie standing quite still behind her as if waiting for her—and remembered as she did so that there had been no mention of the car she was supposed to have the use of, nor any other offer to make provision for her welfare. Stubbornly, and trying not to let her spirits sink at the gloomy, almost menacing quiet of the house around her, Sara told herself that Paul Merinard's continuing absence (she hoped) would be quite enough provision for her welfare to be going on with. And she had better pick up the suitcase and typewriter he had left near the door, and ask Marie to show her around. If she showed her sympathy for the old housekeeper, Sara thought to herself firmly, they might start to get on better, and she would *not* allow herself to imagine that the house, as well as the old woman, disliked her being here!

Three long, quiet days later, Sara could review the situation and decide, ruefully, that if the house didn't dislike her being here, the housekeeper certainly still did.

It was amazing how much deafer Marie could be towards Sara than she had been with Paul Merinard—and it wasn't just accent either, she knew. Her French might be northern but it was near-perfect, and she took care to speak slowly and politely.

It wasn't that Marie was openly hostile. She did everything Sara asked her to do—when she could be persuaded to understand. She had taken her all around the house, opening up empty room after empty room—it appeared that Mr Halberson had spent his last years occupying very few of the rooms of his villa. His bedroom—which she looked in very quickly and with careful respect before asking Marie to close it up again—had a bachelor sparseness; and a shadowy quality from the firmly-closed shutters served to remind Sara that he had probably died in that narrow bed. There was no reason for her to poke about up there, thank goodness, since he seemed mainly to have *lived* in his study, with occasional forays to a formal dining-room for his meals.

The study was total chaos. It was a largish room and filled with heavy furniture—a desk, an armchair, a side-window—and everywhere one looked there were papers, in piles and heaps, under ornaments and paperweights, sticking out of the tops of drawers, jammed in the back of cupboards...Books piled the floor, with more pieces of paper thrust between the pages. Whatever else James Halberson had been, he wasn't tidy. Sara had already come across a used medicine glass and a dirty cup and saucer under the piled-up papers on the desk.

It had been a job, at first, to persuade Marie that the shutters across the study window should be left open: the old woman had muttered about the sun fading the carpet—as if there was much carpet visible!—and had come in and closed them every time Sara left the room. It was a minor annoyance, but Sara had persisted, and finally won, and had even managed to wrench the weathered wood of the window-frame itself so that the window would both open and close again. Marie seemed to have a passion for closing shutters everywhere in the house, which was one of the things which lent the villa its oppressive, stuffy air, and Sara was growing used to walking through shadows everywhere she went: however, she was *not* prepared to use dim electric lights all the time as the old housekeeper seemed to wish. If Mr Halberson had done so, he really had grown odd with old age.

Sara tried not to think about him too much, because she could all too easily imagine an elderly emacitated figure shuffling from room to room, perhaps with the tapping of a stick...She opened the study windows, and her bedroom windows, to let the air and light in and dispel imaginary ghosts; and wished with some wistfulness that the view from the open windows was a little more cheerful. From her bedroom on the first floor, it was trees and more trees, though the sound of traffic from the road reached through them and was somehow comforting. From the ground-floor study, she could see a neglected patch of grass, undergrowth, and then trees again. If the old man who had opened the gates for them really was the gardener, he didn't seem to do very much!

The sea must be out beyond the study window somewhere—but she hadn't let herself explore the garden yet. In fact she had spent these three days in determined, unremitting work. If Paul Merinard should come back, he would find his employee hard at work—and pale, sunless, and dusty, Sara thought dispiritedly as she glanced longingly towards the glint of sunlight visible on the rough grass outside. Here she was on the Mediterranean coast and all she had done so far was walk about inside this shadowy house...upstairs to her drab, heavily-furnished bedroom; into the dining-room to eat Marie's quite exceptionally dull and badly-cooked meals; across the hall again into the dusty jumble of the study. She hadn't even managed to make any visible difference to it yet, either—except for clearing the top of the desk so that she could make different piles there for bills, letters, scribbled notes and what appeared to be bits and pieces of an old printed monograph on chemical mixtures. She had worked during the day, then on into the evening, and gone to bed as early as ten o'clock to lie on her hard bed feeling tired but not sleepy, and trying not to hear the creaks and groans of the old house and ghostly whispering of the trees. Inside the house it was permanently cold. Outside...

It was ridiculous really that she hadn't gone outside yet; had allowed herself to be sucked so totally into the atmosphere of the house. Her head was beginning to ache from constantly peering at different pieces of paper and making out the French written in different and often semi-legible handwritings. Sara knew, with a sudden flash of sanity, that she was being quite stupid in letting Paul Merinard's taunts get under her skin so much that she had been determined to work and work to prove him wrong. Even *he* couldn't expect her to have no time off at all. Here she was, in the middle of an afternoon which smelled *warm* outside, sitting stuffily in an old man's study *making* herself be busy, with work which could just as easily be done after dark when there was nothing else for her to do anyway. Her heart lifted with a sudden sense of liberation. What should she do with her afternoon, then? Catch a bus into St Raphael from one of the autocar stops she had seen at frequent intervals along the road while Paul Merinard was driving her here? It couldn't be far, as it had taken them so little time to drive—or should she go less far than that, simply to Boulouris? It would be pleasant to sit outside that café she had spotted, and drink a café-au-lait or a citron pressé while she reassured herself that there *was* still a functioning world outside the confines of the Villa Robinet. She would have to go into St Raphael sometime, anyway, to do various bits and pieces of shopping, including some typing paper so that she could list all the documents she found under various headings. That could be counted as work, so Paul Merinard could scarcely criticise. However, perhaps she shouldn't choose that today when it was mid-afternoon already and she wasn't sure of the bus times...

But she *could* go to the sea. Sara jumped up; and when her movement scattered a pile of papers she had just carefully arranged, she left them where they lay in a sudden fit of rebellion. Yes, she would go to the sea, indeed she would: first she would go and see if it could be reached from the garden, and if that proved impossible, she'd walk down the road a little way to the nearest of the little coves. She ran upstairs on suddenly light feet and snatched the bikini she had brought with her out of one drawer, a towel out of another, and slid her feet into flat sandals. A cotton skirt instead of the efficient pleats, and a cardigan to put over her shirt in case it was breezy: she was ready.

She started her exploration of the garden simply by stepping over the sill of the study window, only a foot from the ground. At once the sun hit her, so that she lifted her face in wonder to its sudden warmth, and hesitated, tempted to spread her towel out on the grass right here and sunbathe. It was almost unbelievable that the chill inside the villa had been shutting out *this*. A warm current of air caressed her face and arms and, all at once, she could identify the sweet spicy tang in her nostrils as coming from the pines. Beyond the trees, she could almost *feel* the presence of the sea. The villa must be on a small headland and perhaps there would only be cliffs to frustrate her—but she crossed the small lawn and found an overgrown path leading off into the undergrowth.

After a few yards it darkened, with the trees shutting out the sun above her; their great trunks blocking her way until she found where the path wound on between them, with brambly scrub to scratch her shins. The path dipped abruptly, flattened, dipped again round a large tree-surrounded rock whose redness was streaked with grey. And then, suddenly, she could see a blue flash ahead and below—and another—and the path curved round another rock and turned into broken-edged steps cut out of the rockface, leading down. A few seconds of scrambling descent brought her onto a flat rock jutting outwards, still in shadow;

but, straight ahead of her, the sun struck blindingly on blue sea and a curve of white sand. Sara caught her breath. Oh, but it was *beautiful*...

A tiny, perfect, empty arc of beach lay only a few feet below her. Another headland reached out beyond, this one with trees clinging thickly to it, shutting off the little bay into privacy. Glancing round, she saw the 'Private' notice nailed to a tree on the path she had just left—though it looked as if the beach itself could only be reached from the sea, *except* by the path. Perhaps in the tourist season people did land here to swim, sunbathe and picnic; but for the moment, wonder of wonders, she had found her way to the Villa Robinet's own personal beach. She looked round quickly for a way to scramble down, and found more steps cut into the side of the rock: a second later she was on sand, kicking off her sandals to feel the grittiness of it between her toes, running on it, returning breathless and laughing to lean against the warmth of a sun-soaked rock and stare out to sea. To the horizon, it was empty, a sweep of such vivid blue that she had to blink and shade her eyes. On the side she had come down, the red rocks fretted out into the sea, sharp-edged and too jagged for easy climbing, but adding to the beauty of the scene with their depth of contrasting colour. On the other side the headland jutted out, steep-sided, to shut off any further view. Even from above no-one could look down on this secret cove because the trees grew thickly to the edge of the high cliff above.

It was certainly private enough to change in, and Sara swiftly shed her clothes and slipped into her bikini. She undid her hair and shook it out too, revelling in the freedom, careless suddenly of the way her curls cascaded wildly over her shoulders in an untidy mass. The sheltering cliffs reflected the sun's heat back to her, glowing into her winter-pale skin, making her marvel that it could already be so hot in April—she would have to put sun-tan cream on her shopping list for St Raphael.She flung her clothes and towel into the shelter of a rock and ran to the edge of the sea to dip a cautious toe into the water. Brr, it was cold—not warmed up yet from the winter's chill—and she decided, with a chuckle, *not* to be brave and leap into it. She would paddle, and then sunbathe. But the depression of the last few days which had been growing in her was magically lifted; and she decided all at once that it was time she sent Bet a post-card to tell her that she was here safely and, although not *quite* the job she expected, it wasn't going to be too bad after all. She wouldn't, perhaps, mention Paul Merinard—though she might try to describe him, in distinctly unflattering terms, in a letter later on...

Half an hour later, Sara was lying face-downwards on her towel in the middle of the beach, feeling a drowsy contentment at the warmth of the sun on her back. London, and the cold, and even Dennis Mather and her so-called broken heart, seemed a satisfactorily long way away. Now that she had found her way down here, the Villa Robinet and its shadows had receded into ordinariness, so that she could think that the job really *was* quite reasonable, and if it was a pity she had never met Mr Halberson after all, she was still doing something useful by sorting out his papers. Nothing could be bad with the sparkling sea so near at hand; St Raphael to explore later; perhaps Fréjus and its Roman ruins too, on another free day. Mr Halberson's papers might even prove interesting once she had broken the back of the initial chaos. With sleepy humour, she decided that breaking the back of chaos really was too mixed a metaphor for a hopeful writer, and wriggled contentedly on her towel, then raised her head a few inches to adjust her position.

She was suddenly aware of a pair of black, shiny shoes at her eye-level, three feet away from her head. And dark-clad legs rising from them. Before she could do more than gulp, a familiar voice spoke.

'Good afternoon, Miss Farrow,' Paul Merinard said drily above her head. 'I came over to see how you were progressing...'

CHAPTER THREE

Sara swung herself round to a sitting position so fast that for a moment she felt dizzy, sun, sky and sea swinging around her in a blur. She dipped her head to her knees hastily, her hair falling round her face in a curtain; then raised her head more slowly, shaking her curls back with an unconscious gesture. He was still there: unfortunately she hadn't dreamed him. Larger than life, looking normal, though jacketless, with the sun striking blindingly off his white shirt, Paul Merinard stood reprovingly over her—watching her like Nemesis, Sara thought bitterly.

'How—how did you know where to find me?' Her voice came out with husky defensiveness as she squinted up at him, trying to adjust her eyes to his figure outlined against the sky.

'Marie saw you from the kitchen window, so she could reassure me that you hadn't simply vanished into thin air in the middle of your work.'

His voice still had that same dryness, and it stung Sara into a retort. 'Then presumably she could also tell you that it's the first time I've stirred from the house for three days! I didn't know that she was watching me particularly, but she must have been aware that I haven't been out at all, until now!'

'Yes, she did mention it, actually.'

'Then there's no need for you to—' Sara broke off: he hadn't, in fact, criticised, except perhaps by his tone. She tried to stifle her confusion and return to the dignified composure she had vowed to keep in his presence; though that was less easy because she was suddenly aware of the way she was dressed. Or *not* dressed: her bikini, so suitable for sunbathing, was skimpy enough to be the next thing to nakedness. In front of anyone else it wouldn't have mattered, but there was a quality in Paul Merinard which made her far too aware of the picture she must present. She hugged her arms

84

round her knees and tried to feel less self-conscious. 'If you'd care to go back to the house,' she said stiffly, 'I'll get changed and come up and show you what I've been doing—'

'There's no need. It didn't look as if you'd made much progress so far. I merely wanted to see that you have everything necessary for your work, and were finding your way around all right. We can talk about that down here, just as easily as up at the house.'

'Yes, I have got everything, thank you. But—' she broke off again; *but*, she had wanted to add, it would be a great deal easier to discuss that with him if she could reach her clothes, several yards away beside a rock, let alone the fact that sitting at his feet trying to look up at him was giving her a crick in the neck. She could hardly say either of those things. 'But I shall have to go into St Raphael to do some shopping,' she added rapidly, 'so I *shan't* always be at the house. I hope that seems perfectly satisfactory! I seem to remember that you did tell me to organise my own working hours!'

'Of course.'

'And may I see round the Lorivel works sometime? So that I can have a better idea about the business papers I find?' She had already had that idea, though she was saying it now simply to have something to ask him. Squinting up at him, she finally managed to bring his face into focus, and saw him frown.

'I don't know if that will be necessary. We're going through a busy period just now.' His eyes gazed down at her unreadably—but a second later she saw a flash of sarcastic humour in them, and when he spoke again it was with a silky smoothness. 'You know, Miss Sara Farrow, you are beginning to surprise me? When I telephoned this morning to say I'd call this afternoon, I wondered what to expect. To find you half-clad on the beach was...inevitable, perhaps, even if obvious. But since I came down here, you've first of all offered to get dressed, and then chosen to sit in a *most* uncomfortable position—almost as if you genuinely wished I would go away! I wonder why? You are, after all, dressed to show off most of your attributes. Admittedly I was rather surprised not to find you topless when that's such a common habit along this coast—or did you think it would be more effective if you sprang to your feet and that *very* small clip at the back burst open at a convenient moment?'

'Oh!' Sara, who had been listening to him in growing anger, abandoned her immediate instinct to leap to her feet and glare at him, just in case the clip on her bikini bra did give way with the sudden movement. She knew it would be useless to tell him that she hadn't known of his telephone call, and that Marie had delivered no message: he would never believe it. Annoyance at his mocking conceit all at once conquered caution, so that she composed her expression and found herself answering him in a careless drawl.

'It's just that when I saw you, I realised why you didn't actually attract me at all! Besides, you're so very conceited that it—it stops being amusing, you know?'

'Re-ally?'

'Yes. You see, it becomes boring if one can't surprise someone. I'm sure you can understand that. Admittedly, I thought... But then when you arrived, I decided no, it would just be the same old thing all over again—'

She knew as soon as the words were out that it had been a mistake to play up to him, and it made her break off, wanting to take the words back. Without his having moved a muscle, she could feel a current of danger coming from him which sent a tremor along her spine. She made herself sit still and finish her statement with a shrug which, even to her, felt false. He said silkily,

'So—I don't attract you in the least?'

'No, you don't! On the train it would just have been someone to talk to pass the time, so it wouldn't really matter. But—' Sara suddenly felt breathless, and suddenly realised how thoroughly alone they were, which made her finish rapidly, '—I really don't believe in mixing business with—with anything else—'

'Inconsistent,' Paul Merinard murmured mockingly, and was down beside her on the sand in a swift movement. His hands, hard and warm, imprisoned her bare shoulders, holding her effortlessly as she tried to twist away from him. '*Much* too inconsistent to be anything but another game...No, I shan't let you go, Sara, why should I? It's such a conveniently private spot that you've chosen to flaunt your beauty in, so why should I waste it? So...I don't attract you at all? And you don't intend to make *any* move in my direction? And you really don't believe in mixing business with pleasure...?'

Between the softly-spoken words his lips were caressing her cheek, the line of her jaw, her throat. Sara, held helplessly by his strength, could only gasp, the words with which she should have answered him lost in a confusion of sensations. Quivers ran along her skin from the touch of his lips and her whole body seemed to come alive. When his hands left her shoulders she sank back, pliant to the hand which slid round behind her head and tangled in her curls, to the fingers which moved under her back to move her close to him. His shadow blotted out the sun as his mouth came down hard on hers, hungry, demanding, kissing her with a bruising force which sent liquid shivers down into her abdomen. Her lips parted under his, to the probing of his tongue, swept by a tide of passion too unexpected to be resisted, and when his weight shifted to lie across her she let out a tiny unconscious moan. His mouth moved against hers more gently, and one hand came round to cup her breast, the tiny scrap of material which had covered it loosened and moved away to let his fingers find the rosy bud and caress it.

Sara's body twisted against him as pleasure shivered all through her, all consciousness and reason drowned in instinct, responding to his lips and hands with an abandon she had never felt before. The hard male hunger in him was palpable, sending currents of an equal hunger coursing through her blood and sweeping her in its tide. She was lost in the power and attraction of the man—lost, but knowing it was an attraction he felt too, that there was a chemistry between them as powerful as it was unlooked-for. She didn't care that anything might happen, here on this isolated beach: the moment was too strong, and the attraction which held her in its grip, making her want to belong to him, only to him, totally. She clung to him—and then suddenly, before she knew it, he was gone.

The shock of it was so intense that for a second she couldn't move. She was aware that he had let her go, rolled away from her, stood up. It was like being doused in cold water, so that the heat of the sun suddenly felt like a thread of ice along her skin. It was also like waking up, from a dream into cold reality. It was a reality which held a sudden intense loneliness, so that she wanted to call out 'Paul!' and have him come back to her; but it also held shame, and the knowledge of where they were, and who they were. How *could* she have responded to him like that, after all his mockery, when she didn't even like him? And how could he have made her respond, then dropped her, uncaring? She felt the sharp sting of tears in her eyes as she fumbled hastily, with clumsy fingers, for the straps of her bikini top, and told herself that they were tears of anger; and then she heard his voice. It was filled with the same sardonic mockery as ever—even if there was an undertone of savagery in it which suggested that the passion he had been dis-

91

playing hadn't left him totally unmoved.

'Whose point have we proved—yours, or mine? I warned you not to play games with me. But, as it turns out, *I'm* the one who chooses not to mix business with pleasure!'

He walked away. She was aware of his going, out of the corner of her eye she watched as the tall figure retreated towards the path; but she couldn't find her voice until he had reached the first of the trees. Even then, she couldn't find anything suitable or dignified to say, because the words which came out were instinctive.

'I *hate* you—'

A dry laugh came back in answer, to prove he had heard her. She was afraid for one brief second that he would take it as a farther challenge and come back, so that she jumped up and on hasty, stumbling feet made for the rock where she had left her clothes. However, the voice which came from somewhere invisible above her said merely, mockingly, 'You still have an unbreakable contract—Sara!' And then, as she drew a long, shaking breath, she could hear his footsteps retreating on the path above.

The beach lay as warm, as empty, as beautiful, as it had an hour ago. The sea was just as blue. The sky was cloudless. Sara, looking round at it all, trying to get it into focus, told herself that what she was feeling was only fury. She remembered with bitterness that Betty had tried to warn her, had seen her as an unsophisticated dreamer and had worried about her. Certainly it was true that nothing in her life had prepared her for a man like Paul Merinard and the potent attraction he could switch on at will.

Well, she was prepared now, she told herself angrily. With her lower lip caught between her teeth, she fought determinedly against the desire to run away, to leave the job and the place and the man and let him sue her for breach of contract if he dared. It would be cowardice and she *wasn't* going to let him bully her and frighten her away. She would, however, take all the care she could never to be alone with him again...and whenever she *did* have to come face to face with him she would treat him with an icy composure. Paul

Merinard, she decided, was such a typical example of 'Bet's wolves' that he wasn't even worth thinking about, he was a...a minor irritation, to be ignored! And, she thought vengefully, if he assumed he'd proved to himself that she was too brainless to do anything other than sit and moon over him because he was rich and handsome and very obviously *spoilt*, he'd soon find out how wrong he was.

Caution allowed that she should stay on the beach long enough for him to have left the Villa Robinet; but when she reached the house she slammed straight into the study, found herself a large empty sheet of paper, and sat down to draw herself up a proper work schedule. She would give herself a certain number of hours each day for work, and the rest of the time would be her own, including whole days off since she was entitled to take them. If she chose to put in her working hours after dark and enjoy the daytime sun she'd do that too—though she'd go further afield to the public beaches in future, she decided—and whether Marie minded it or not, she'd reorganise mealtimes to suit herself. When the chart was worked out to her satisfaction she rang for Marie, pressing the bell-push beside the desk which she had never dared to use until now, and when she appeared in the doorway told her with cold politeness that she wished to be informed in future if ever there was a telephone message for her. She even showed the housekeeper the chart, telling her that it would be pinned to the wall so that Marie could see when Sara planned to be in or out. And, as a further move towards efficiency, Sara requested that the pile of old grocery boxes she had seen in a back room should be brought in here so that she could clear everything out and stack it—and then clean the room.

Marie's reaction to that was outrage, and a flood of resentful complaint which seemed to consist mainly of the fact that Mr Halberson had insisted the room was never to be touched, so it never should be. Sara, trying for patience, pointed out gently that Mr Halberson was now dead; and received one of the housekeeper's deaf, malevolent stares before the old woman turned and shuffled away—anger and resentment clearly visible in every line of her body. Marie would have to comply if Paul Merinard ordered it, Sara knew...but she also knew that she didn't want to have to appeal to *him* for help. Well, she would just have to do the job herself, and if possible choose Marie's day off to do it in: she had already learned that the housekeeper always went off to see relatives on alternate Saturdays. And if finding the job done, and finding that Sara had dared to venture into the kitchen in search of cleaning materials, provoked an outburst, then so be it.

Looking round, Sara realised how tentatively, and amateurishly, she had been working so far. She drew another piece of paper towards her and listed things to buy which included wallet files and clips, drawing pins and folders, notebook, pencils, and stick-on labels—for all of which she would keep careful receipts and send them to Paul Merinard as expenses.

Or rather, to Lorivel, to keep things as impersonal and official as possible. When, later the same afternoon, Sara was called to the phone and found herself talking to Lorivel in the person of Paul Merinard's secretary, she felt that the impersonal approach had been decided on by both sides. And so much the better. The secretary was ringing to sort out the details of Sara's pay, telling her it would be paid by banker's draft at the Credit Lyonnais Bank in St Raphael and would arrive there fortnightly so that she wouldn't have to wait too long for her first paycheck. Sara found herself wondering whether that was what Paul had in fact come to tell her—if he hadn't been distracted...

She had been a little surprised to find his secretary sounding like a practical middle-aged career woman: it would have been more in keeping, she decided nastily, if he had surrounded himself with young leggy brunettes purely for decoration. But she was *not* going to think about him. She certainly wasn't going to feel a betraying quiver inside herself at the memory of the beach. He was physically attractive—so what—so were lots of people. Grimly she decided to allow herself only the hope that if Lorivel *was* going through a busy period as he'd said, that would keep him away from her. Apart from that thought, she was just going to *forget* him.

CHAPTER FOUR

It was less easy to forget him when she came across a family tree showing all the Merinards from a great-great-great-grandfather down to the present day—which she decided confirmed her idea that he was spoilt, because it showed him as an only son and, according to the chart, the last of the Merinards in direct line. She saw that he must have inherited Lorivel when he was twenty-seven, and that he was thirty-two now. She noticed that his English mother, Pandora, Mr Halberson's niece, had died two years before her husband.

It was the earlier Merinards who interested her most, she told herself firmly, because they were the most relevant to the history of Lorivel. She saw that the very first one was marked as being a pharmacist, and it was easy to imagine how he might have experimented with perfumes as a sideline which, by the next generation, had turned into the main business. Sara filed the family tree away carefully, resisting the temptation to visualise all those early Merinards, how they lived, what they felt. There was plenty to catch at her imagination—but she must be disciplined, and concentrate on facts.

She came across some photographs which aroused her curiosity too. There was a batch of them showing old buildings and people working in the fields, but it was two others, put away separately and more carefully than Mr Halberson's usually untidy filing methods, which drew her attention. They were pinned together but had obviously been taken generations apart, because the older one had faded to sepia and had been taken against a very artificial studio background which looked somehow Eastern. Both were portraits of young women, dark-haired, pretty, and with a very faint likeness between them which might have made Sara conclude that they were Mr Halberson's wife and a grand-daughter, if she hadn't known that the old man was a bachelor.

The modern portrait looked recent and showed the head and shoulders of a young girl with a charming, lively expression and long brown hair falling to her shoulders: she stared out of the picture with an artless innocence which made her appear very young. Turning it over thoughtfully, Sara saw a sad message scrawled on the back in the old man's hand— 'Ysabel—died, aged twenty' with a date almost five years ago. The name, with its Y at the beginning in the old Provencal spelling, suggested she might be French, but she couldn't be a Merinard or Sara would have noticed it on the family tree. She wondered who the girl had been, scenting somehow a romantic story in the careful putting-away of the two photographs.

She tried, on impulse, asking Marie about them—but the old housekeeper first affected a fit of deafness, then burst out with a real anger that it wasn't any of her business, nor Sara's either, nor *anyone's*, to go 'poking about amongst monsieur's things' with so little respect. There was a sing-song quality in her

101

voice which was almost frightening before she lapsed abruptly back into her usual flat, resentful tones to say that she must go and make tea now for Monsieur Julien the gardener because it was one of his working days. Monsieur Julien's idea of work was to smoke his pipe, drink tea, and pull up the occasional weed— but as he looked about eighty that was hardly surprising, and he was at least pleasant and had given Sara his toothless grin whenever she saw him.

The villa was as quiet as befitted a geriatrics home, Sara decided wryly. She was glad to escape from it for a day in St Raphael. The town turned out to be easy to reach by an hourly bus along the coast road, with a friendly, chatty, middle-aged driver who reminded her of the Parisian bus drivers of her childhood, and who was prepared to tell her what to see in the town and that there was a big daily market every morning, which was in the old part of the town, further inland and beyond the railway line. Sara loved markets, particularly French ones, with their enormous, elaborate displays of every different kind of food—

reflecting the passionate interest most French people took in eating.

St Raphael's market proved to be as lively as most, with, especially, a mass of fish-stalls displaying the local catch, everything from flat-fish to rouget, heaps of tiny silvery whitebait, prawns and lobster, navy-shelled mussels, even shark. There were also great banked-up stalls of flowers which made Sara long to buy arm-fuls of them to take back to brighten up the villa. She didn't, because it would have meant carrying them around all day; but by the time she caught the bus back along the coast road in the early evening she was feeling light and contented after her hours of sunny freedom.

She had bought all the stationery she needed, and had sent off a postcard to Bet, and another to the Gaunt Press staff, at the same time as she sent off all the stationery receipts to Lorivel with what she hoped would show prompt efficiency. She had been consciously happy wandering about all day exploring, seeing the contrasts of the old and new areas of the town, watching the boats in the small busy harbour in the middle of the town's seaboard, admiring the deep glowing colours of the cathedral's stained-glass windows which, a notice told her, were modern ones to replace those blown out in a bombardment at the end of the Second World War. She had lunched at a pavement café, eating a toasted sandwich and drinking coffee as she watched the world go by, basking in the sun and in the pleasure of being back in her beloved France. She had felt a little wistful as she wandered round alone, and had found herself wishing her job wasn't so isolated: particularly she had felt wistful at the sight of all the elaborate Easter confections behind the plate-glass windows of the chocolate shops, everything from giant eggs spilling over with chicks and sugared flowers to tiny nests full of sugar almonds.

Easter was only twelve days away, and she couldn't help remembering what a family celebration the 'Jour de Pâque' was, and that she would be alone for it. But she was used to her own company. She had felt half inclined to join up with a bunch of young Dutch students on holiday whom she had met on the beach, and who had been thoroughly willing to be friendly, but she had found herself remembering Paul Merinard's critical comments and hadn't made any promises to meet up with them again. She was here to work—and besides, they were all very young, and she didn't really want to go to a party over at their camp-site at Fréjus and get back so late that it would annoy Marie still further.

The day after tomorrow, Marie's day off, she would get the study cleaned out—and that would be annoyance enough for the old housekeeper. It was a pity that she couldn't have brought her some fresh fish from the market to vary Marie's offerings of watery soup and tough, unidentifiable meat...But somehow even the sight of the Villa Robinet's heavy, gloomy gates couldn't daunt Sara as she jumped lightly down from the bus and stood for a moment appreciating the warm air, and the golden light striking off the red castle on the tiny island half a mile out to sea. It really did look like a golden island in the evening sun—'L'Ile d'Or,' which gave this area its name—though it didn't seem to have a particularly romantic history, as far as she had

been able to discover. It simply lay there looking decorative against the blue sea. Sara knew,
light-heartedly and with a sudden sense of
triumph, that she was glad to be here in spite
of everything. A three month contract went
both ways, and if *she* was tied to it, then Paul
Merinard couldn't stop her enjoying being on
the Esterel coast either.

Her day in St Raphael had brought another
bonus. In an agency window she had seen a
coach tour advertised which had a 'trip round
a famous parfumerie' as its main attraction.
The Parfumerie wasn't Lorivel, but one of the
larger, less exclusive ones; and although the
trip would be no more than the standard
tourists' quick look round, Sara had decided
that it would be worth doing. If she wasn't
to be shown round Lorivel she would at least
see one of the others, she decided defiantly,
and had gone in and booked one of the few
free seats which were left. She could even be
picked up outside the Villa Robinet instead
of having to go into St Raphael to catch the
coach, as it would be coming this way so as
to include the spectacular Corniche views as

part of its trip. It was to be in the middle of next week, and she was looking forward to it. She marked it off carefully on her work-chart as a 'free day'—and if she was going to be cleaning all day Saturday, she thought, she was entitled to it!

As it turned out, it was most definitely a relief to be out of the Villa when the day came round—even though the weather was beginning to break, with the cold chill of a mistral beginning to blow, and spoiling the run of sunny hot weather just in time for the Easter Bank Holiday which would bring the first flood of campers and caravanners to the coast. It was a relief because Sara's spring-clean of the study had brought such a flash of rage from Marie that she almost expected to find herself locked out of the house every time she left it— or even to find the stairs greased to make her fall and break her neck, she thought with a wry attempt to make a joke out of it. There had been no further sign of Paul Merinard, though Sara would almost have welcomed the sight of him as a counter to the sullen silence Marie was now adopting and to the sinister, creepy feeling that the housekeeper was sitting in the kitchen crooning spells to herself. As she stood shivering by the side of the road waiting for the coach to appear, Sara decided grimly that if she *did* up and leave, and Paul Merinard *did* sue her, she could produce genuine grounds for complaint, so she needn't really worry too much about that. Her working conditions had been appalling from the start and it might even wipe the conceit off his face if she stood up publicly and said so. On the other hand, she was beginning to find the Lorivel papers interesting—and she was already feeling a tug of fascination at the thought of building up a picture, like a jigsaw-puzzle, out of the wealth of old letters and notes and articles which Mr Halberson had stored up over the years.

She exchanged a wave with the young English manager of the caravan site opposite as he appeared to paint up his 'Vacancies' notice for the Easter weekend: she was used to seeing his chunky fair-haired figure over there as she came in and out of the Villa. Hearing him talk with a cheerfully appalling French accent, she had discovered that he was an expatriate Englishman down for the season, and they had taken to exchanging casually amiable greetings. His name was Ted and he had the job of overseeing a small army of young girl cleaners who cleared out the permanently-sited caravans between rentals, and who were, he had told her disgustedly, 'all about sixteen and all clueless'. She mimed a shiver at him as he waved back at her, and he mimed back casting his eyes to heaven with a wry shrug. Then the large cream-coloured coach Sara was expecting swept into view, and Sara climbed up into it as it stopped for her.

The trip provided a commentary from the young coachdriver which he produced in a continuous patter while he drove—with almost unnerving casualness—along the twisting Corniche road which rapidly became so spectacular that the journey became a matter of wonder. For the next hour Sara's eyes were filled with images of villages perched on the edge of rocks, castles, vistas of pine-trees and sea, precipitous drops and craggy, rearing mountains—with even a glimpse of the high snow-clad Alps in the far distance as the coach swept down from the high Corniche to the flat, fashionable outskirts of Cannes.

From here, they would turn inland to go up to the pottery town of Vallauris for an early lunch, and then climb on inland towards the high ground and Grasse, set amongst the hills and the acres of flower-fields which belonged to the various parfumeries established there. The grey skies had stopped mattering many miles back as the coach passengers craned to look out at a wind-whipped sea beating itself spectacularly against red crags hundreds of feet below the steep edge of the road; or exchanged exclamations and laughter at the sight of the modern Porte la Galère perched on a headland, its strange bulbous architecture looking like nothing so much as a set of weird mushrooms; or listened with sudden seriousness as the driver explained how a tree-blight had scarred the pines away from the hills in their thousands so that patches of bare hillside showed the sad damage.

Sara, who had been given a seat next to a boy who turned out to be German, found herself pressed into translating for him, and then for his parents too, since the French commentary was too fast for them and they understood her English better. By the time they stopped for lunch she had been thoroughly adopted by both the German parents and their tall seventeen-year-old son, and they all agreed when criticising the vulgar commercialism of Vallauris which, even if Picasso *had* once lived there, had since obviously developed a much less attractive personality.

Later, as they piled into the coach again and went on upwards amongst the rising heather-clad hills and twisted through the narrow streets of villages, Sara had to try to convey the coach-driver's often ribald comments on 'all the beds Napoleon had slept in' because this was the Route Napoleon, which she remembered from the history books she studied at school. She had almost forgotten about Lorivel as the coach lurched round several sharp corners and a notice announced that they were entering the small, busy hill-town of Grasse. As the coach drew up oppo-site a large clearly-marked factory which was their destination, and the passengers began to climb down, the first thing that struck her was that the whole air was perfumed, on a wave of flowery sweetness. The aura was so strong that it must make the whole town constantly aware of the factories in its midst; small and large, they vied for fame and competed with each other for custom, pumping out a sweet-scented air as they processed the flowers and shrubs brought in from the fields. The driver shepherded his flock across the courtyard towards the glass doors of the entrance and Sara looked round her curiously, wishing she was more than an ordinary tourist so that she could see what went on in all the different buildings which stood looking as bleak and matter-of-fact as if they produced something as mundane as...paper-clips, instead of sweet-smelling luxuries.

Inside, the reception area was almost disappointingly like that of any other large office or works, with glass doors, a few secretaries visible behind typewriters, and a few people in white coats wandering around; though as a door opened along a corridor Sara was intrigued to catch a glimpse of a laboratory with people bent over long benches full of scientific-looking glass containers. She moved to go closer, but was firmly rounded up to join the rest of the party by a white-coated guide as they were shepherded through a doorway into what was described as the 'museum area'. They were only allowed in the public areas, the guide said pointedly, and then the tour proper was beginning with a description of some examples of old machinery on show.

Sara had to concentrate because her German friends had smilingly elected to stay with her instead of waiting for a German-language tour and she had to do her best to listen and translate at the same time. Along with everyone else, she tried turning the handle on a heavy wooden tub which, apparently, had been the method for drying rose-petals; she studied a massive metal press which had once been used for crushing out flower oils; and murmured over a vat of wax which came entirely from bees and already held the aroma of the flowers on which the bees had been fed. There were large photographs blown up to poster size on the walls, showing people in old-fashioned aprons and headsquares picking in the flower-fields, reminding Sara of the pictures she had found in old Mr Halberson's study. She felt that she ought to have been taking notes of everything that was said—but that would have made her too conspicuous and besides, she had the translating to do as well, which was sometimes difficult. The guide swept them from one exhibit to another pointing out an old centrifuge here, demonstrating an oil-base for keeping perfume longer on the skin there, and giving a quick dissertation on the seasonal growing of different flowers and shrubs.

She wished there was more time for questions, but the guide rattled on at high speed, leading them round the large hall, then through a corridor into another room where she showed a glassed-in corner laid out as a miniature laboratory. This was an example of a place specially used for 'mixing'—the combination of different perfumes to produce a compatible whole, which then became the recipe for a particular product. Only an expert could experiment with the mixtures, and only the most expert could find a new blend to produce a new and original perfume. Sara would have liked to know more about that, but they were swept on again to be shown different 'perfume carriers'—spirit, wax, oil—and sprayed perfunctorily with a spirit-based after-shave which left a pleasant aura in the air; and then the instructional part of the tour was abruptly over as they were ushered into a sales-hall the size of a ballroom with a polished wooden floor, chandeliers, and counters ranged round all the walls. This, after all, was the point of letting tourists in—not to show them the parfumerie's secrets, but to get them to buy samples of as many products as possible.

Every conceivable product was on show, from elegant cut-glass bottles of the most expensive perfume to brightly-coloured scented candles, from bath-oils and aftershaves to scented cards to put away in drawers amongst your clothes, everything in such profusion and so beautifully presented that it was difficult for anyone to go away without having bought at least something. Sara managed to resist the temptation to buy anything at all though she was tempted by the little pots of perfumed beeswax, mainly because the pots themselves were so pretty. Most people were buying, and taking their goods to a counter to be wrapped in bright striped paper with the parfumerie's name clearly printed across it. At last the coach driver reappeared and began gathering up Sara's party—and Sara suddenly found herself being presented with a jasmine-scented candle which the German boy had bought for her. When she protested at the gift, he told her with a grin that it was for all her hard work in translating for him, and *particularly* for the Napoleon jokes.

They were both laughing as they strolled back across the courtyard and crossed the road towards their coach, clearly labelled with its tour name in the narrow street. As they approached it Wilhelm slipped out an arm round Sara's waist, and she turned to make a teasing comment to him—and then froze. A pavement's width away, and staring at her with a thunderous expression on his face, was a tall, dark, familiar figure. Sara's heart slipped a beat.

He seemed to have emerged from the restaurant doorway directly behind him, and had perhaps been lunching there—a long lunch, since it was already three o'clock. There was no hope of avoiding him, and Sara's guilty jump had already made Wilhelm glance round in surprise. She reminded herself quickly that she had no reason to feel guilty, and she was perfectly entitled to be on a coach trip to Grasse if she chose; but she found herself muttering, 'It's my boss,' to Wilhelm as she hastily detached herself from his encircling arm. Paul Merinard was already moving towards her with an unnecessarily grim expression on his face.

'What on earth do you think you're doing?'

'I'm on a day trip,' Sara said defensively. She looked past him, at the tall, dark, elegant woman who had been standing beside him and who was now plainly waiting for him, and added pointedly, 'Please don't let me disturb you! We're just going back—'

'You came on that coach?' His eyes flicked to the package in her hand with a look of exasperation, and Sara thought crossly that if

117

he was angry because she ought not to be buying anything but Lorivel, he was taking competitiveness too far. 'Of all the foolish—well, you can withdraw from the rest of the trip, and *I'll* drive you back. Don't argue! Say goodbye to your *friend*, and tell him to tell the coach driver you've made other arrangements, and join me over there!'

It was impossible to argue with someone who had already walked away. For a moment Sara was tempted to ignore his high-handed orders and get into the coach, but decided that he was perfectly capable of coming and hauling her out of it. She gave Wilhelm a helpless look as he stood there looking both disconcerted and embarrassed, and said rapidly, 'I'm sorry. *Will* you tell the coach driver for me? And—and please tell your parents it's been lovely to meet them! I have to go—I work for him, you see!'

She gave a wry shrug, trying to smile but with anger sparkling in her eyes, and turned away to where Paul Merinard stood waiting. He wasn't bothering to look and see if she *did* obey him: he was busy saying goodbye to his companion, kissing her affectionately on both cheeks and holding her hand with every evidence of close friendship while she made a smiling protest at his departure and told him not to forget that they had a dinner-date next week. She was a woman of about his own age, Sara saw as she came up to them, dressed with that definably French chic which looked carelessly confident but contrived to show off impeccable taste. She gave Sara an amused, curious glance which with one delicately raised eyebrow took in her yellow cotton trousers, chunky woollen jacket, and hair tied back in a childish ribbon. Paul, on the other hand, totally ignored her while he finished saying his goodbye—just as if she were a lost dog he had called to heel. Sara thought angrily—and finished with a silky, '*A bientôt*, Louise, and do forgive me, please,' before he bothered to turn round to Sara as Louise walked away.

'My car's round the corner. Come along.'

He had already set off with his long-legged stride, so that Sara had to save her breath for keeping up with him. She hadn't missed the fact that he and Louise had conversed with the intimate 'tu' of very close friends, so that she felt more than half inclined to make some pointed remark about spoiling his afternoon: she decided not to, but it provided a satisfactory stiffener against her involuntary inclination to notice that he looked as handsome as ever. And, she reminded herself quickly, as bad-tempered as he had the very first time she saw him on the station platform in Paris. He stopped dead beside a car and gave her a withering look as she almost bumped into him. It was enough of a reminder of his usual attitude towards her to make Sara find her voice.

'I don't know what all this is about, but if you want to talk to me, you can do it without driving me anywhere! In fact—'

'Get in, and don't argue. This is business. And put that—whatever it is, out of sight!' With an angry gesture which made Sara's jaw drop, he seized the package out of her hand and threw it into the back of the car. She could only stare at him, startled, and then clamber hastily into the front seat as he looked as if he might throw her in, too. He slammed the door, walked round, got in himself, and started the engine, giving her an exasperated look as he said, 'Are you really too ignorant to realise that as a Lorivel employee, you shouldn't be going round another parfumerie? You'd better tell me at once if you asked too many questions, or tried to go anywhere you weren't supposed to go!'

CHAPTER FIVE

'No, I didn't!' She'd been tempted to, but she certainly wasn't going to tell him that. 'That's *ridiculous*,' she said, almost wanting to laugh.

'No, it isn't, and I don't want to be accused of sending spies in to my competitors!'

'Industrial espionage in the perfume business?' Sara couldn't help the words coming out on a giggle. 'You can't mean—I'm sorry, but it just sounds so silly!'

'It seems so to you, does it?' His voice, even in those few words, was clipped and angry, and Sara realised abruptly that he *did* mean it, and her own words, to him, must have sounded both crass and rude. 'It's a highly competitive business, and since every parfumerie has its jealously-guarded secrets it takes very little to cause a scandal, or the rumour of one! Whatever you and I may know to the contrary—'there was a heavily sarcastic note in his voice—'just think for a moment how it could look. Suddenly I have a new employee, but I keep her tucked out of sight down on the coast. The next thing you know, she's innocently going round a rival firm, amongst the careful concealment of a batch of tourists. Now, *if* you turned out to have internal knowledge, a science degree tucked away in your background perhaps—'

'I haven't!' Sara interrupted hastily.

'—or if you'd simply been told what to look out for, you could make *my* behaviour look extremely unethical!'

'I'm sorry,' Sara said stiffly. 'I was just—I didn't think of it. You wouldn't let me see round Lorivel, so—' She gave him a look which tried to be apologetic as well as cross, though as he was keeping his eyes on the road as he drove, her gesture was inadequate. 'Nobody could possibly think you'd sent me in there as a spy,' she pointed out, 'considering that you picked me up the moment I came out of the place! I mean, you'd have pretended not to know me, wouldn't you?'

'Quite,' he said drily—so drily that she stiffened in sudden comprehension. 'As I said, it takes very little to start a rumour, but I hope there won't *be* any rumours!'

'Well, I'm sorry to be wasting your time!' When he made no answer to that, but continued to thread his way through the traffic in the narrow streets, Sara went on in a nettled voice, 'What on earth would I be supposed to be looking out for, anyway? Secret formulas?'

'Every parfumerie has them, naturally. Above all—as I'm sure you're not too stupid to know—each parfumerie has experimental work going on!'

'Well, we certainly didn't go near anything which looked at all secret, in there! And—and I'm sorry, but you should have told me!' She looked curiously at his grim profile, seeing him suddenly as the head of a busy, competitive business instead of simply as the man whose behaviour had tormented her ever since she arrived. She found herself abruptly aware that behind the almost sultry darkness of his good looks, he looked tired as well as cross. Almost as if he might have been working too hard.

'What kind of experimental work?' she asked curiously.

'Several kinds. New solvents—new carriers—ways to make a perfume last longer on the skin—ways to prevent skin acidity changing the balance of a blend. All the obvious things, about which you appear to be so ignorant! Then of course,' he went on before Sara could protest that she hadn't got far enough with Mr Halberson's papers to be anything *but* ignorant, 'there are the externals. New forms of packaging, new designs. And when it comes to spying, even the details of someone else's marketing campaign could be of value—if a rival firm wanted to slip in first and launch a similar campaign a few weeks earlier!'

'I—I see.' Sara hadn't thought of any of that: she knew she should have, but it hadn't occurred to her. She remembered the 'mixing' laboratory, and added thoughtfully, 'And each firm must be experimenting to invent new perfumes as well, I suppose. Looking for something different, to catch the public's attention.'

'Quite,' he said again.

'I can see that there *would* be a lot of secrecy

125

involved. Though I shouldn't think anything important's left lying around, is it? And is it really so—so cloak-and-dagger?'

'One does well to keep it in mind.'

'Oh. Well, I'm sorry, and I didn't mean to cause trouble. I just didn't understand, that's all!' She gave him a quick, half-shy look as the car picked up speed down a hill which led out of the town, with a vista of bumpy moorland spreading out before them with flat fields showing up here and there. She remembered, with sudden wariness, that she had been thinking of him as an enemy—and decided as quickly to forget it. She couldn't *quite* forget the magnetism which, even now, made her heart give an unwary thump; but she wanted to put that aside and go on asking him about the parfumerie business, since he seemed more communicative than usual. She was framing a question when he spoke again abruptly.

'Shall we have some music?' He reached forward to turn a knob on the dashboard with one firm olive-skinned hand. 'Oh, by the way, my secretary's given me those expenses chits of yours. If you need any more stationery let

126

her know and she'll have it sent down to you: I should have remembered to tell you to do that in the first place!'

She wasn't going to apologise again: after all he *hadn't* told her. She wondered if it was the right moment to raise the trouble she was having with Marie, but there was another subject she wanted to press first. 'If you could get your secretary to have me taken round Lorivel,' she suggested, 'it would be a great help—'

She heard him say, 'Yes, I'm sure it would,' on such a sardonic note that she might have objected—but for the fact that her attention had been diverted away from him, swept into a flood of memory by the music which was pouring softly from the car radio. She had known without noticing that the dancing strings were playing a familiar air, but now the clear reedy sound of the oboe came in, every note, tone and phrase an echo from the past. The Corelli Concerto—she had heard her father practising it so often that it took her straight back to childhood. Concerts...her father playing, her grandfather conducting. The recording, surely this same one, which her grandfather had kept and which she now had safely at home. She was aware of Paul glancing at her: then the music was ending, and an announcer's voice came through smoothly to say that they had been listening to a recording by the late Justin Farrow. And now there would be a short talk on the... The broadcast was cut off abruptly as Paul leaned forward again to flick off the switch.

'Sara? Is something the matter?'

'No, of course not. I was just sorry not to have heard the rest of the music,' she said quickly.

'You like that kind of thing?' He sounded surprised: surprised enough to bring a sharp reply to Sara's lips, though it was mainly a defence against sudden wistful memories.

'Why shouldn't I? Not everyone prefers disco music!'

'No, I don't, for one. I've got a different recording of that, a more recent one, by—' He broke off, and she saw him frown. 'Farrow? Justin Farrow wasn't a relative of yours, was he?'

'My father. And it isn't bias to say that your

recent recording can't be as good as his!'

'No, I don't suppose it is. He must have died when you were a child, surely. And *his* father was—'

'Carl Farrow the conductor, yes.'

'Hm. You're surprisingly well-connected for a—' He broke off, but went on before Sara could speak, swinging the car smoothly into a sharp left-hand turn, saying, 'I think we'll avoid the autoroute and take the country road. I'm sure you'd like to stop and look at the view, wouldn't you? Justin Farrow's daughter and Carl Farrow's granddaughter—well, well! You can't be working for the money. For what, then—a sense of adventure? Or just to stop you getting bored? Or have you got expensive tastes, which make you need extra cash?'

'I don't know why you should assume grandfather was rich! And my father's royalties all go to a Music Scholarship, if you want to know!'

'Oh dear, a poor little orphan?'

'No,' Sara said between her teeth. She didn't know why he had to sound so unpleasant about it, or even if he knew how that phrase could grate, but she was scathingly angry. 'No, a long

129

way from that! My grandfather may not have left me much money, which isn't surprising considering he had heavy expenses—including the expense of bringing me up! But what he *did* leave me was a great deal of love...and standards *you* wouldn't understand! I don't know why you have to treat me as if I was a—a cross between the village idiot and Mata Hari, but I can only suppose that *you* were brought up be such a spoiled *brat* that you were never taught to see other people as human beings, or to value them not for what they owned but for what they could do!'

She knew she had startled him by the way his eyebrows went up: she had startled herself, too. He pulled sharply off the road, onto a gravelled strip obviously designed for people to park and enjoy the scenery, since the ground fell away from here to give a magnificent sweep of wild hilly moorland dropping to the silver of a lake in the distance. It might have been a romantic spot to stop, in spite of the still-grey sky above them and the wind whipping the heather below, but Sara was too angry to notice. Or to care. As he turned towards her she gave him a glare which ought to have stopped a rhinoceros in its tracks. He didn't make any attempt to touch her. He said merely, drily, as if they were having an ordinary conversation,

'If you feel like that, why aren't you studying music? With your heritage, it's what anyone might expect!'

'I didn't happen to be born with any musical talents.' That had hurt, when she was young: there were too many people who did expect her to have inherited at least an aptitude. It had taken a lot of gentleness and encouragement to stop her minding. Sara lifted her chin, unconscious of the way pride gave her an almost regal dignity which presaged the woman she might one day become. 'You don't have to feel sorry for me,' she said coldly, and with a touch of scorn. 'I can make my own career. I don't suppose you'd understand *that*, either—but what matters is "the pursuit of excellence", in *any* form. That's what my grandfather used to say, and I believe him!'

'And in your case...?'

'In my case, I intend to be a writer! What

else do you think I'm doing here?'

'You know, you almost convince me?' He sounded surprised—and Sara, who had been so wrapped up in memory that she had almost forgotten who it was she was talking to, came back to the present and gave him a swift, suspicious look. 'I wonder...? No, *don't* glare at me like that, and I do understand "the pursuit of excellence", believe me! What else makes one go on trying...? Believe it or not, I can also guess what it might be like to be born into a famous musical family without any talents of your own. Musical talents,' he said hastily as Sara opened her mouth to retort. 'It would be like being born to a parfumerie without the nose, wouldn't it?'

'*Nose*?'

'It's an expression. It means...oh, the ability to sense what will mix, and what won't. The talent for blending which has to be born in you and can't be learned. I was lucky: I *did* inherit it. My father, too. Great-uncle James, he had all the technical knowledge in the world, but he couldn't manage more than a simple blend. Uncle Robert, my father's

132

cousin, was the same. He's only just retired as the firm's accountant, and he could do anything with figures, but perfumes? No.' He was sounding so much more human than Sara had ever heard him that she could scarcely recognise his voice, with that note of friendliness in it. 'As for valuing people for what they can do, Sara—I have a man working for me now whose father is a peasant straight out of the fields, but his son is our best blender. Besides me. And that isn't conceit, it's luck!'

'And hard work and application?'

'Those too, but luck first. And as for your question about whether things are really so cloak-and-dagger...a few months ago Jacques Peyre's father was suddenly offered a farm of his own. Out of the blue, with no apparent strings attached but an "anonymous sponsor" in the background. Two of my research assistants have been offered very good jobs elsewhere in the last few weeks. And when we wanted to replace a secretarial assistant we had a remarkable number of applications!'

'Goodness,' Sara said weakly, fascinated by this side-light on the non-ethical side of business competition. 'Does that always happen? Or—' she looked at him with sudden interest— 'are you working on something special?'

He gave her an unreadable look, and she wondered briefly why she sensed disappointment in it: perhaps it was just a silly question. 'What parfumerie isn't?' he countered, watching her. 'And in particular, of course, every parfumier ever born wants to produce a new classic—a great perfume which will last for generations without losing its popularity.'

'Like Chanel No 5, you mean? Sorry,' Sara said hastily, aware of tactlessness, 'I really don't know much about—'

'The complete amateur? Yes, it will do as an example—though naturally I'd rather you'd have said "Lorivel 3" or "Pandora". The really great perfumes are rare, but both those two *are* classed as classics. My father was responsible for both of them, and they're still our main international sellers. But, I was saying: if a parfumier thinks he *is* on the verge of producing something which could turn into a classic, the last thing he wants—out of pride, as well as for commercial reasons!—is to have his work pirated!'

'Yes, I can see that.'

'Or even to have the launch details of a new perfume leaked, and its publicity undercut.'

'If it was really good—a classic—wouldn't it stand on its merits?'

'Yes, perhaps, but advertising always helps. There's a risk attached, in any launch. Should we do market research when that means sending out samples which could be stolen, or have enough faith to go into full production without it? Should we decide on advance publicity or keep everything under wraps until the last minute? Has anyone produced anything in too similar a style in the last six months? What shall we call it—a number, or a name? And *what* name?' He was speaking almost to himself, as if these were questions he had gone over many times before; but as Sara looked at him curiously his attention came back to her. She was aware of a touch of amusement in his eyes for her interested expression as he said drily, 'I'm not giving away any secrets, you know. All those questions apply quite generally!'

'But Lorivel *is* working on something new?

On a new classic?'

'Does rumour have it so?'

'Obviously rumour does, or you wouldn't have had all those suspicious things going on!' She felt the fascination of it, the excitement which must come with the invention of something special and rare, and longed to know whether it was his own work, or that of the other blender he had mentioned, Jacques Peyre; or did the two of them work together? Something in Paul's expression made her add quickly, 'All right, I won't ask! But surely—when you've got so many parfumeries grouped in one town, it must be very difficult to keep things completely secret! You can't really mean that everyone in Grasse goes round suspecting everyone else!'

'No: those of us who work in the same area, and know each other, are particularly careful to respect each other's privacy. Of course a great deal is known or guessed, and word goes round; but the trouble normally comes from outside.'

'It would be the worst thing of all to have a special formuala stolen and copied, wouldn't it?' Sara said thoughtfully. 'Like—writing something really good, and then seeing it come out under someone else's name before you could do anything about it.'

'I'm glad you can see that.'

'Well, of course I can!' She looked at him in surprise. 'If you're in the middle of something like that, I'm amazed you ever employ strangers at all—people like me, I mean!'

'It was done in a hurry, certainly, and without sufficient thought. The idea was to keep great-uncle James thoroughly occupied, but without offending him. I suppose I didn't really believe that Matthew Gaunt would find me someone so promptly, but when he did...' He shrugged, though his eyes remained consideringly on Sara's face, with an expression in them which she couldn't quite fathom. Sara was suddenly aware that she had been liking him—and respecting him too—and finding something to like in him was not only surprising but, somehow, dangerous. She stirred a little, and tried to keep her mind firmly on old Mr Halberson.

'I thought he never went out—your great-uncle, I mean!'

'Now and again he'd hire a car to bring him to the works, usually when we least expected him. I don't believe he ever went anywhere else. He liked to feel he was still part of the place. To write the history—which *is* all history, so you're not likely to find anything secret in it!—would have given him something to do. But, as it turned out—'

'As it turned out, he died, so you needn't have worried about it. Only,' Sara said, puzzled, 'why did you insist on keeping me on?'

'Why shouldn't I keep you on, Sara, when you're so decorative?'

'I don't care for empty compliments, thanks.' She wished that the silky, mocking note hadn't crept back into his voice, when they had been getting on so well.

'Not at all empty. You *are* decorative. Just the sort who might be expected to appeal—'

'I'd rather be noticed for my intelligence— wouldn't *you*?' She asked the question pointedly, staring him out—but feeling a sharp regret for the fact that he was lapsing back into his

138

old manner. While the intentness of his gaze sent the inevitable quiver along her nerves with a betraying reminder, she remembered too, abruptly, that he was capable of making a game out of seeing how far she would react to him. The landscape around them suddenly seemed far too empty, the car far too private.

'That's an interesting statement,' he said conversationally. 'By the way, who was your friend? The one I had to tear you away from?'

'Friend?' She was confused for a moment—and then realised who he meant, and remembered at the same time that *he* hadn't been alone when they met, either. 'Just someone I met on the coach,' she said shortly. 'Why, who was yours?'

'Louise? Just someone I've known for a long time. Jealous?'

'*Jealous?*' She gave him a stare of angry disbelief, feeling with annoyance the way the colour came flooding up into her cheeks.

'I just thought it might have aroused your competitive instincts?'

Sara tried to give him a withering look—which was so unsuccessful at withering him

139

that he merely looked more amused than ever. She burst out, '*Why* must you always talk to me as if I was—'

'Perhaps because it amuses me to see you blush? I didn't think anybody did that any more. You puzzle me, you know. Either you're such a good actress that you ought to have taken it up professionally, which does at the moment seem unlikely—*or* you might be a complete amateur drawn in unaware. It will be interesting to find out. But I don't mind admitting, Sara, that you're *very* bad for my powers of resistance...'

His hand was sliding along the back of the seat, with obvious intent. There was obvious intent in the look in his eyes, too. When a sharp blast on a car's horn sounded loudly behind them, out of what had been total emptiness a moment ago, it was almost funny. It was even funnier to see the large, familiar, cream shape of a tour coach edging up beside them, with the recognisable figure of the young coach-driver cheerfully talking as he slowed to let his passengers appreciate the view. Sara's former tour was taking the country roads too—and she remembered that they had had been promised a 'scenic inland route' for the return journey. She was aware of curious eyes peering down at *them*, as well as at the moorland, and bit her lip on an involuntary laugh at the sight of Paul's expression, both disconcerted and annoyed. It was such an unlikely Sir Lancelot arriving out of nowhere to rescue her...and then she was aware that Paul's arm was drawing her against him, and that he was saying smoothly.

'Let's give them something other than the Lac de Saint Cassien to look at, shall we?'

She could have pulled away from him, in front of all those witnesses. She told herself that she only didn't because it would look un-dignifed, and what was a kiss, after all? He could hardly go any further than that with a whole coachload of people looking on...As he bent his head to hers she knew that pride ought to have stopped her kissing him back, but somehow it didn't, as his lips caressed hers with surprising gentleness: she knew that she hadn't the sense she was born with as he drew her unresistingly closer with the kiss deepening into hard passion. She was gasping when he let her go, and as her lids fluttered open she was aware of his heart beating under her hand, echoing the wild clamour of her own. She was still cradled against his shoulder, his dark eyes looking down into hers, his breath uneven against her cheek.

'All honey and sweetness.' There was a rough note in his voice. 'I wonder, do you give as much as you promise...? It's a pity I have to go back to work—but I do!'

'Then you'd better!' She wanted it to come out tartly, but instead her voice was husky. She sat up sharply, drawing away from him, suddenly and embarrassingly aware of the coach, Wilhelm and his parents, the fact that she must have been perfectly recognisable to the whole tour party. She had told Wilhelm that Paul was her employer, too, even if all the others would simply have assumed he was her boyfriend. She cast a distracted glance round—to see the road empty beside them, and to hear a dry laugh from Paul as he caught her eye.

'Oh, our audience has gone. It's not because

of them I have to go back to work! Here—
have your hair ribbon.'

He handed it to her, and started the engine
as coolly as if she had been a minor distraction. As no doubt she had, Sara thought bitterly, knowing that she ought to be able to treat
the episode in the same way. A kiss was
nothing. Paul's habit of mocking her was
nothing, too. She certainly wasn't going to let
herself feel hurt by it: she wasn't going to feel
that there ought to have been something else
between them to give meaning to the chemistry
which drew them together so powerfully. She
pulled her hair back sharply and yanked the
ribbon into a knot round it, then huddled into
her corner keeping her face averted and telling
herself sarcastically that when he said 'go back
to work' he probably meant 'go back to
Louise'. A lady who was obviously more than
a friend. The moorland unrolling on each side
of the road gave her an excuse to look out at
the view, and after a moment she said stiffly.

'It's almost as beautiful here as the coast.
We drove up the Corniche this morning, and
it's quite magnificent, isn't it?'

'Yes, very striking. I find all that rugged grandeur a bit obvious after a while, though: I prefer the mountains inland. I suppose, because I grew up with them.'

'What did you say the lake was called?'

'The Lac de Saint Cassien.' They were driving round the edge of it now—a wide silver sweep of water with islands in the middle of it, its surface ruffled by the wind and a splatter of rain. A few small boats bobbed at anchor at one end of it, near a wooden building which announced itself as a yacht club. 'It's useful for boating and picnics, not for swimming, though. There are bird sanctuaries on the islands.' Paul's voice was casual, and didn't alter as he added, 'Oh, I see we're about to pass your friends again!'

Sara had already noticed the coach, moving slowly while the driver no doubt gave the history and recent use of the lake. Her faint feeling of embarrassment at the sight of it made her turn defiantly, as they passed, and give a cheerful wave. She didn't see whether anyone waved back because they swept past too quickly, but the gesture had been for Paul's benefit as much as anything. He was looking quite unmoved as she glanced at him, in fact he started humming gently under his breath as he negotiated a sharp hairpin bend and then turned onto a wider road signposted for Fréjus. He appeared almost to have forgotten she was with him. Sara wrenched her mind away quickly from its tendency to dwell on the almost Grecian perfection of his profile, and made herself think about Lorivel instead, and her interest in what he had told her. After a moment she said thoughtfully, 'It *must* be difficult to think of a name for a new perfume, when just about everything's been used before. 'I suppose "Pandora" was named after your mother. That must have—'

'And how did you know that?'

'Well, it's fairly obvious!' She cast him a surprised look for the sharpness of his tone. '*That* can't be a secret, surely! And there's a Merinard family tree amongst Mr Halberson's papers. Not,' she added pointedly, 'that I was all that much interested in the later members of the family, compared with the earlier ones!'

'Ah, I see. Back to the history again. I

thought you were sounding surprisingly know-ledgeable all of a sudden. And what's your next question going to be? Shall I tell you all about Fréjus, which you can see we're just approaching? Or do *you* want to tell *me* something?'

'Yes, I do, as a matter of fact!' Fréjus could be left to a study of the guidebooks and, Roman city or no, it looked singularly un-attractive as they came into its outskirts which were full of tall and ugly blocks of modern flats. Since he had given her such a good open-ing, Sara decided it was a convenient moment to make an attack on his self-satisfaction. 'I've got a complaint to make about my working conditions!'

'Oh really? What—'

'Marie. I've *tried* to be tactful with her, but she resents my being at the villa so much that it's becoming impossible! And the study I was supposed to work in was filthy, but she hates me even more now I've cleaned it! I know she's old, but she's also extremely *peculiar*. I won't bother to mention that the food's awful, and getting so much worse that I'm likely to starve—but as for the rest of it, since you *are*

146

my employer, I think I'm entitled to ask you to do something about it!'

'And what do you suggest I do?'

'Well, *speak* to her!'

'Nothing else? Not move you up to the Lorivel works—?'

'Well, I know you're not likely to do that, don't I? After all you've said today? I'm not completely stupid!' Sara gave him an exasperated look which, all too suddenly, held the pain of wishing that he *would* treat her as something more than a stupid but kissable doll; that he would see her as a human being. 'I'm just asking you to talk to her!' she said, into his frown.

'Yes. All right. I will.' The car picked up speed suddenly: she was scarcely aware that he had slowed down. They were threading their way through undistinguished back-streets which surprisingly quickly turned from the edges of Fréjus to the edges of St Raphael and streets Sara could recognise. Paul seemed to have withdrawn into a thoughtful, narrow-eyed concentration; but when he spoke again his voice was surprisingly friendly. 'Yes, all right,

Sara, I'll talk to Marie for you. I suppose she *has* got rather odd without anyone noticing. She was with the old man for so long, and looked after him so thoroughly, that I suppose his death might have been too much of a shock for her. She was always fiercely protective about him.'

'It's not that I can't understand it. But it's not just old age—Monsieur Julien's perfectly normal!'

'And still pretending to garden twice a week? I can't really sack him, even though he's far too old to do much: he used to work in the fields for us and he's more or less an institution. I think we've been paying him a Lorivel pension since my grandfather's day!' Paul gave a grin of reminiscence—and Sara, who had been watching his face when she might have been looking out at her favourite parts of St Raphael as they drove through them, found her heart turning over very suddenly at the mischievous, youthful expression it gave him. To see him smile like that, without his normal sardonic look, was...she pulled her thoughts up sharply, confusedly glad that he was watching the road and not looking at her, and found something to say.

'Maybe I should ask Monsieur Julien some questions, if he's been with Lorivel such a long time. He must remember all sorts of things!'

'You can try. I'm not sure if you'd be able to get much out of him: he's even deafer than Marie. It really interests you—the past?'

'It's what I'm here for, isn't it? Even if Mr Halberson is dead, I can try and sort out as much of the story as possible! I wonder—? Even if Monsieur Julien can't hear me, I could probably ask him by signs if he knows what some of the photographs are! What sort of date they were taken, that kind of thing. He'd recognise the buildings, and the fields, wouldn't he?'

'I could probably tell you what they are, if you show them to me sometime.' Paul made the offer easily, with the same friendly note in his voice which was so surprising, and so surprisingly sudden, that Sara didn't know what to make of it. He glanced at her, and added with what was *almost* the old mockery, but not quite, 'Don't look so puzzled, Sara!

I can be quite helpful when I try, you know!'

'Yes, I—I'm sure you can.' She wished there wasn't a part of her telling her not to trust him, warning her to remember how nasty he could be, reminding her that his magnetism was something he usually chose to use against her. She certainly wasn't going to start imagining what it would be like to fall in love with him— was she? No, of course not! She thought of a question, and although she tried to make her voice conversational, it came out abruptly. 'Who was Ysabel? Spelled with a Y at the beginning, and—'

'*What*?'

It had been the wrong thing to ask. She could see that at once, as all the friendliness was wiped from his expression leaving a cold taut mask. She almost flinched at the way his hands tightened on the wheel and the car gave a sudden spurt of speed. 'I'm sorry,' she said rapidly, 'It was just a question, forget it—'

'No, *you* can forget it! And that'll teach me to—' He broke off, his expression nothing short of murderous. 'Sorry to disappoint you, but there's nothing for you there!'

'Wh-what? Look, I'm sorry,' she said again, shaken by the icy dislike in his voice, shaken too by regret for something which seemed to have slipped unwittingly out of her grasp. 'It was just a photograph I found! I know she's dead because it was written on the back, but I didn't know—'

'That there was an old scandal to be raked up? Really?' The words sounded scornful. 'Just a photograph, was it?'

'Yes! Two photgraphs actually—one old one, one modern one with—with this girl's name written on it. They were put away in the desk drawer. I found them, and I wondered who they were, that was all!'

'All right, then, I'll tell you.' But his voice wasn't any less cold. 'I'd forgotten great-Uncle James was so fond of her—or that she reminded him of some lost love or other! Her name was Ysabel Renard, and she was accidentally drowned while swimming. She was twenty years old. And she was, at the time of her death, my fiancée. There's nothing secret about it, and nothing to be learned from it—except that the very young can be very foolish.

151

And,' he said between his teeth, 'I suggest you tear up the photograph, along with any ideas you may have had.' The car squealed to an abrupt halt: with a feeling of unreality, Sara realised that they were outside the Villa Robinet's gates. Paul turned his face towards her to give her one comprehensive look, which somehow had an almost brutal sexuality in it to remind her of their earlier encounters. As she opened her mouth to say something—anything—he added,

'Stick to your other efforts in future, they are at least amusing! Alternatively, of course, you could stick to the job I'm paying you to do, instead of running round the country cuddling tourist boys! Now get out!'

The scorn in his face and voice suggested that it would be useless even to answer him. Sara, dazed into shock by the violence of his reaction to her innocent question, stumbled out of the car and felt it begin to accelerate away while her hand was still closing the door.

How could he change like that, from one mood to the other, just because she had said something to upset him? She could be sorry to have brought up something which obviously still hurt him, even after so many years—since it *was* almost five years since the girl Ysabel had drowned—but there was something more than that behind his anger. It was almost as if he thought she'd brought Ysabel's name up deliberately to taunt him with it...but why on earth *should* she? It was like groping in the dark trying to understand his moods, Sara decided unhappily.

She refused to analyse why, in particular, she was unhappy rather than angry, and made herself shrug. So he had driven off in a rage—so what? He was only the man she worked for, a man she hardly knew, a man she didn't even *want* to know any better. There was small hope now that he'd try to do something about Marie's behaviour, because he had obviously forgotten all about *that*, in spite of his promise to help. But that had been before she mentioned Ysabel.

As she pushed the gates open to walk up to the house, she wished fervently that she *hadn't* mentioned Ysabel, or even found the girl's photograph.

CHAPTER SIX

As a day, it had been a strange mixture. An hour later it descended into nightmare.

Afterwards Sara could scarcely believe it could have happened—nor the way her life could change so abruptly afterwards. Even a fortnight later she was still looking back with disbelief, and telling herself that it had all been too gothic to be true.

By then, she wasn't sleeping at the Villa Robinet any more—though she was going there each day to work. It wasn't Paul Merinard who had plucked her out of the Villa's sinister surroundings, either: Sara had seen nothing of *him* since the afternoon he had driven away in such a rage. She had had no communication with him, either. She told herself she was glad about that; in fact she was stubbornly determined *not* to communicate with him. If he cared to find out that she wasn't living at the Villa Robinet any more, but on the caravan site opposite and amongst a host of new acquaintances and at least one friend, *then* she would tell him clearly and graphically why. But she certainly wasn't going to get in touch with him and complain. And she didn't think Marie would dare...

The nightmare had begun, that afternoon, with a gesture of apparent normality from Marie, even if it had seemed unexpectedly helpful. She had told Sara that there was 'a big box of papers' up in the attic, forgotten until now; would mams'elle care to go up and look at them to see if they were anything important? In Sara's dispirited state, it had seemed at least a distraction. She had followed the old woman upstairs, then up a further flight of narrow, uncarpeted stairs she hadn't even noticed before because they were tucked away at the end of a dark passage. It had seemed slightly odd, after Marie had unlocked a heavy wooden door with a large old-fashioned key, to be told that there was a light-switch at the far end of the dim, triangular, junk-filled room under the eaves whose features could be made out only by the light from a cobwebbed skylight; but Sara had stepped obediently inside, firmly quelling a feeling of spookiness. And after that...

Even the memory gave Sara a shiver. Marie had certainly meant to do what she did. There could be no accident about the slamming of the door, the turning of the key. And, even if the shadows in her mind might have cleared later and made her change, she had meant, at the time, the dreadful sing-song crooning threats which came clearly through the locked door to Sara's horrified, disbelieving ears, and which still made the back of her neck prickle when she made herself remember them. She would leave mams'elle there to starve, and that would teach her; it was no use knocking because nobody would hear; she was caught now, and would soon be dead like the other one; maybe Marie would burn the house down because there was plenty that would burn, oh yes, and that would look like an accident, now wouldn't it? And more of the same, going on and on...And then, with even more sinister implications, silence.

Sara could tell herself now that it probably *had* only been meant to frighten her—to frighten her into going away altogether, once Marie had released the heavy lock and let her out. That she had certainly meant to leave her there for some time was proved later by the fact that Marie had put on her hat and coat, locked up the house, and gone out for the rest of the afternoon and evening, when she normally only left the villa on her day off.

At the time, Sara knew ruefully, she would probably have panicked marginally less if she'd known the housekeeper *had* gone out, because it was much worse to think that she was locked up in the top of the house with a mad old woman below threatening arson. She could remember now in a shamefaced way how she had hammered on the immovable door with a steadily rising hysteria; and with what desperation she had dragged a trunk full of clothes under the only other way out, the skylight. She couldn't really remember how she had managed to force the skylight open and scrambled out of it—though she *could* remember rather too vividly sitting on the steep pitch of the roof sobbing because there didn't seem to be any way down. Somehow it didn't occur to her at that point to scream for help, only that she must get down somehow before the mistral increased and blew her off, or the rain which had been spattering all afternoon made the roof so slippery that she'd fall off anyway if she tried to move. And if she *did* fall from this height she'd break at least a leg, and lie there unseen amongst the crowding trees. Paul Merinard was the only person who knew she was at the Villa Robinet at all and *he* wasn't likely to come looking for her...

Rescue took an unexpected form. She'd forgotten all about the caravan site opposite, steeply-stepped up its slope to give a clear view through the trees of the roof of the Villa Robinet. She had certainly forgotten about Ted, the young, cheerful, English caravan-site manager. He said afterwards, with a practicality which made her giggle a little bit too much because the memory of her fear was still with her, that he could hardly have missed someone in bright yellow trousers, and it had seemed just that bit too eccentric to imagine she might have decided to sunbathe up there on the one day when it was cold and rainy. He turned out to be very good at coping with a girl in strong hysterics, and thoroughly practical about drainpipes and ladders. He had seen Marie go out, too. After he had got Sara down, and they couldn't get into the firmly-locked house because Sara's key was still on the inside, he had taken her over to the site, calmed her down, and said grimly that she'd better stay in one of the empty caravans overnight and he'd come with her to the villa in the morning. It still made Sara feel slightly sick to remember standing on the doorstep with Ted beside her the next morning and watching Marie's expression crumble into fear at the sight of her—because, to her at least, the disbelief which preceded it suggested that Marie had believed her to be still locked in the attic...

Sara shook herself, glad to come back from memory to present sunlight. The greatest relief of all, somehow, was the knowledge that the chunky, practical Ted had totally believed her from the beginning and had shown an elder-brotherly protectiveness which was immensely comforting. It was still comforting now to know that he would certainly come looking for her if she didn't come back from the Villa after a day's work—and although, at Sara's urgings, no open accusations had been made, Marie must certainly know that. Not that Marie was showing any signs of making further trouble—in fact the old woman's broken, cringing manner nowadays made Sara feel almost guilty. Perhaps the crisis had even shaken her out of her shadowy world of incipient madness, because she seemed both aware of what she had done, and terrified that retribution would follow. It was that which had made Sara feel she could go on working at the Villa—as long as she didn't sleep there.

She'd had an argument with Ted about that. He'd wanted her to ring up Lorivel instantly and resign: he'd even offered to take her on as an extra cleaner on the site if she needed an alternative job. Sara, herself, wasn't quite sure why she was so determined to go on working on the Halberson papers—except for the feeling that she would miss something important in her life if she didn't. Also, she wasn't going to be beaten. She had, however, accepted with alacrity Ted's suggestion that she went on sleeping on the site, assuring him that she didn't mind at all if he put her in with one of the young cleaning-girls because the empty caravans were gradually filling up with pre-booked rentals. In exchange, she'd offered to help out on the site when she wasn't working at the villa. In fact, during the last two weeks, she'd helped out quite a lot—including the Easter holiday, so that it hadn't been the lonely celebration she'd feared, but something more enjoyable in spite of the hard work.

One thing she wouldn't do—stubbornly, determinedly—was make any contact with Paul Merinard, or Lorivel.

Thinking about that, as she packed up her papers after the nine-to-five hours she was now setting herself and prepared to cross the road back to the site for the evening, Sara let out a small sigh.

It was far better not to think about Paul

Merinard at all, except to be glad that she *hadn't* seen him since he drove away in a rage two weeks ago. Almost two-and-a-half, if she was really counting. She should comfort herself with the knowledge that, up at the site, people treated her as an ordinary human being with ordinary human reactions instead of making her feel as if every conversation was a matter of wandering through a maze filled with distorting mirrors. That, somehow, seemed quite a good image for the way it had been talking to Paul. And if she hadn't been in such a bewildered state about *that,* she told herself, she probably wouldn't have lapsed into such an embarrassing state of hysteria later that same afternoon. Surely she wasn't going to let herself feel sore-hearted because his flash of rage with her was beginning to seem like something final.

She let herself out of the villa, crunched her way along the drive in the warm late-afternoon sun, pulled open the big iron gates, and began the now-familiar wait for a break in the increasingly busy tourist traffic whizzing along the Corniche road. With Easter over the number of cars had increased, suitcases on roof-racks showing they were making for holiday destinations, registration discs indicating their owners as Belgian, German, Dutch, French, occasionally English. Sara darted across to the site entrance, with its bright flags hung out, and began to make her way up the steep hairpin road which zig-zagged upwards with tracks running off at each bend to lead to rows of rectangular caravans, some with their own neat gardens marked around them, others simply set amongst rough grass and the many trees which had been left to landscape the site. She caught sight of Ted a few yards away, fiddling with a water stand-pipe which seemed to have developed a leak, and called out a hello to show him she was back. He turned round with a grin.

'Hi, Sara. Everything all right in the witch's castle today?'

'Well, I haven't been turned into a frog, have I?' she responded light-heartedly. 'The greatest danger I'm in is crossing that road morning and evening... Is it always like that?'

'Worse later, they tell me. And if you *will*

do it...' Ted looked for a moment as if he would re-start the argument about her working at the villa; but shrugged instead. As she walked on, he called after her, 'Hey, you're still on for the Saint's Day celebrations in St Raph' tonight, aren't you?'

'Sure. See you later!'

It was amazing how much more sociable her life was now, Sara thought as she climbed up the hill towards the caravan she now shared with a young girl called Ruth. She refused to let her mind drift painfully back to the puzzle of Paul, which always seemed to be there somewhere in the back of her thoughts, and made herself concentrate instead on the fact that it really was very comfortable living here. Even the view from the site was an improvement on the villa: because of the way the caravans had been landscaped into the steeply-rising hillside, she now woke every morning to a sight of the sea, sparkling blue to the horizon, and a vista of pine-clad headland stretching out into the blue with a lighthouse on its highest point. Ruth was one of the 'clueless sixteen-year-olds' Ted had once described to her, and had seemed inclined to be sulky at first about having Sara dumped on her to share her living-space—but her sulkiness had gone once she realised that Sara didn't plan to tell tales on her for the fact that she was supposed to sleep on the site, but usually didn't. She had confided that she slipped off most nights to be with her boyfriend who was a Spanish waiter down in Boulouris, even asking Sara with a grin to 'cover for her' if necessary. And the caravan, though small, had two separate bedrooms, even if Sara's doubled for its living-room, so that one walked directly into it on opening the door. The space was very well-planned, though: the caravan even had its own shower rigged up to the mains water supply, and a powerline for electric light.

There was, Sara decided firmly, a lot to recommend life nowadays. She didn't even have to suffer from Marie's cooking any more, but could eat at the site's cafeteria which was cheap, but very French and very good. As she let herself into the caravan with her key, Sara told herself that she certainly wasn't going to waste her time wondering wistfully why there was still one oddly unhappy area in her life. Why one man had taken such a cold dislike to her...why he had been friendly one moment, icy the next, and had had no communication at all with her since...how he could kiss her as if it mattered to him and then drop her as if it didn't...

She pulled her thoughts up sharply, making herself think instead that it would be fun to go into St Raphael tonight with Ted and the others to see the fireworks and street celebrations in honour of La Sainte Vierge who, apparently, was considered to be the town's protectress far more than the saint who gave the place his name. She knew the others had assumed Ted had moved her on to the site because she was his girlfriend, and her lips curled into a tiny grin of reminiscence; poor Ted, he had taken some pains to assure *her* that he hadn't got any intentions like that in her direction, because he had a steady girl-friend back at home in England and he wanted to keep things that way. She had told him gravely that she quite understood—and had felt like telling him, too, that she was far happier to have him around in a brotherly role than as anything else. She didn't because she wasn't entirely sure he'd take it as a compliment. It was the truth, however—though Sara couldn't help wondering, with a betraying slide to her thoughts, why it was that she never did find herself feeling the least inclination to fall in love with suitable, friendly people like Ted, whereas... In fact, she thought with a slightly wistful exasperation, there must be something wrong with her, because suitable and friendly people like Ted never fell for *her*, either.

She dismissed the self-doubt ruefully, and set about deciding what to wear for this evening. Her jeans needed a wash, and wouldn't be dry in time, so she settled on a sun-dress: it had been hot all day, increasingly hot ever since the mistral had blown itself out a few days ago, and she could take a filmy shawl with her in case the wind off the sea blew colder after dark. Quite a lot later, when she actually put the dress on, she realised that she'd forgotten quite what a plunging neckline it had, and hoped that it wouldn't give Jean-Claude, the young chef from the cafeteria with a roving eye, too many ideas; particularly about trying to untie the laces which kept the soft green material together at the top. Oh well, she thought with a chuckle, she could cope with Jean-Claude, if only by hiding behind Ted— or even, if it came to it, by swearing at him in French in words she was sure he thought her too ladylike to know! She piled her hair up quickly on top of her head as she heard the camp mini-bus give a loud toot down below as a signal that Ted wanted to leave. Seven or eight of the young site-workers were going in together, so it promised to be a cheerful party.

St Raphael was dressed for the festival, with bright lights in the trees and streamers everywhere. The crowds in the streets were good-tempered and children ran about in their best clothes bright-eyed and sucking ice-cream and toffee-apples and Sainte-Vierge sugar fish. Once the procession to carry the Virgin's statue down from the cathedral to bless the harbour was over, most of the shops re-opened and the brightly-lit cafés were doing a roaring trade.

Later, when it was properly dark and everything else had been sampled, there would be the fireworks. There was dancing, too, up in the market square, and the heavy beat of disco music could already be heard in the distance whenever there was a break in the cheers, chanting, and brassy tootling of the town band competing for attention down on the waterfront. Sara, wandering round with the others amongst the jostling crowds, felt as happy as a child, and as full of questions. She tugged at Ted's arm.

'Hey—you see that big batch of German tourists over there?'

'Yes, why?'

'Did you notice, they didn't seem to mind at all when we had all that intoning about La Sainte Vierge saving the town during the German occupation? You'd think they would, wouldn't you?'

'It's all a hell of a long time ago!'

'Yes, I know—but round here, the occupation still seems to get mentioned quite a lot! And nobody ever says that it was actually the Canadians who blew the cathedral windows out during the liberation, they just blame *that* on the Germans too!'

'Didn't know it *was* the Canadians—was it? Anyway, it's all old history, and everybody knows *now* that spending power beats history any day!' Ted gave her a grin. 'Shall we go up and see what the dancing's like?'

They all went, to find the market area as transformed as the rest of the town: if there was still a faint aroma of fish, it was soon forgotten in the flashing disco lights, the tables set round the edges of the square, the wine shops which were also handing out paper cups enjoying a boom in business. Quite a few people were dancing, more sitting down and drinking, often in large family parties which would get up after a while and move off, leaving someone else to take over their table. It was some time before Sara noticed that a new group had arrived at the table next to the one bagged by the caravan-site party, because she was out in the middle of the dancers trying to fend off Jean-Claude's determination to dance close when *she* was equally determined to keep him at a safe distance. Even when she came breathlessly off the floor to plump herself down beside Ted and shoo Jean-Claude off in the direction of Elli who was—on and off—supposed to be his girlfriend, there were too many people milling about for her to notice anything. She took a sip of her wine which she was diluting with Perrier to make it more thirst-quenching, and had turned to tease Ted for being so English as to stick to canned beer when he said, 'Don't look now, but someone over there's taking a great interest in you. I said *don't* look now...yes, all right, he's looking the other way now. Next table, at the end—with that bunch who look as if they're slumming.'

Sara turned her head. She hadn't thought about Paul all evening: she was so used to pushing the whole idea of him away, to relegating him to quite a different compartment of her life, that it came as a shock to see the familiar dark head, the perfect profile. He was lounging easily in his chair with a careless grace which looked, nevertheless, thoroughly athletic, and was laughing at something the woman next to him was saying, smiling down into her face as she laid a hand on his arm. Sara looked away quickly—though not before she'd noticed what Ted meant, because the whole group at the next table had a casual smartness which made them stand out. And not before she'd noticed, too, that he had a different woman with him this time...of the same age and type, but a short-haired blonde with slanting eyes which she was using to great effect.

'Know him?' Ted asked casually.

'Sort of.' She *wasn't* going to say 'It's my boss' this time.

'Very much the rich at play, that lot.' Ted, Sara thought, was trying not to sound curious. 'Oh well, I suppose everybody comes to these things. He was certainly riveted by *you*, though. I felt like going over and telling him to stick to his own side of the fence—except that he doesn't look like someone I'd like to start anything with. Maybe I *will* tell him, at that—'

'Don't be silly. He—he was probably wondering where he'd seen me before, or something.' Sara cast a swift, almost involuntary glance over her shoulder; and then added, meaning to sound light but finding the words coming out with an unnecessary snap, 'He looks thoroughly well occupied, to me!'

'Yes, doesn't he? But he's looking again, now—'

'Come on, let's dance! Oh come on, Ted—don't give me that again about having two left feet—you've only got to stand there and twitch, for goodness sake—'

'Waste of good drinking time,' he grumbled, but good-humouredly, letting Sara pull him out onto the stone flags which made a slightly uneven dancing area. It was almost as if he realised that the reason was what Sara had seen out of the corner of her eye—Paul getting to his feet—when he let her drag him right into the middle of the dancers, and then over to the far side even though the music was positively deafening over there because it was next to the disco amplifiers. The whole dancing area was noisy, but just here it was impossible, and after a few patient minutes Ted mimed putting his hands over his ears and steered her back towards the middle. From

here—though she pretended she wasn't looking—Sara could see that Paul still wasn't in
his place, and told herself that that *didn't* give
her a faint stirring of panic. Then a moment
later she saw him, walking casually back round
the edge of the dance-floor with a couple of
bottles of wine in his hands. That must have
been why he had got up, to buy more wine,
not to come and speak to her at all; and she
couldn't think why she had been so stupid to
suppose that he *was* coming to her. And why
would it matter if he did, anyway? He could
hardly start ordering her about, or tell her to
go home. Sara, keeping a light-hearted smile
pinned to her lips, told herself defiantly that
she had every reason for wanting to avoid Paul
after the way he'd spoken to her last time she
saw him. On the other hand, it would be quite
idiotic of her if she let his presence spoil her
evening.

She didn't know why she hadn't said to Ted,
'That's Paul Merinard of Lorivel,' which
would have been much more reasonable than
half pretending not to know him. Her mind
sought round for an excuse and came up with

the fact that Ted might turn stubborn and take the opportunity to tell Paul about the Marie incident. She could imagine all too well how scornfully disbelieving he might be over it—and how little he would want to have his evening interrupted by the problems of his employees. He was obviously enjoying himself with his so-smooth friends, not least with the female companion who could make him laugh so happily that it made him look quite human...Sara, dragging her mind away from thinking how well it suited him to laugh, decided with annoyance that he could, as Ted had put it, stick to his own side of the fence, and that if he did come across to speak to her, she'd just give him a cold nod and make it clear that she, too, was enjoying herself with her own friends. Or perhaps with luck she could avoid him altogether by making it quite clear she *didn't* want him to speak to her.

'Hey, stop glaring at me. And I'm *not* going to dance to this smoochy number—let's go back and have some more to drink! Your admirer,' Ted said pointedly in Sara's ear as she woke up abruptly, 'is now dancing. So we can do the opposite and sit down, can't we?'

'Oh—yeah. Sorry!'

'You're the only girl I know who can smile and scowl at the same time. Must take practice!' But Ted was grinning, and seemed comfortingly disinclined to make any more comments as they returned to their table. The 'smoochy number' had a heavily sensual beat, and Sara was glad that Jean-Claude had just got up to dance it with Elli, particularly when he gave her one of his best looks before Elli, who was heavy-set and tough-looking but quite good-humoured, gave him an exasperated yank to remind him that he was with *her*.

Ted sat down with all the thankfulness of a man to whom dancing was more labour than pleasure, opened another can of beer, and poured Sara another drink. She took a hefty mouthful of it, and turned quickly away from the dance-floor to make some bright comment—telling herself that she certainly didn't want to watch Paul moving with leisurely grace with his blonde's arms affectionately round his neck as she looked up with smiling animation into his eyes. Some time later, when the beat changed and most of the couples came drifting off the floor, she found herself seized with a sudden chattiness which made her turn her shoulder to ask Ted what time the fireworks were supposed to be, was it eleven-thirty or midnight? She could have sworn that someone hesitated behind her chair, then moved away—and covered a sudden shaking feeling inside her by calling across the table to one of the others that they needed some more to drink, didn't they? And whose turn was it to fetch it? A moment later she had leapt to her feet again and dragged Louis, the camp-site electrician, onto the floor with her to dance again—and if he looked faintly surprised, that was because he couldn't have known that Sara's peripheral vision had shown her that Paul hadn't sat down, but had looked just as though he was making some excuse to his friends to leave them for a moment...

She had thought that the sixsome at the next table might soon grow tired of street-dancing and move on, perhaps to a night-club which would be a more suitable setting for them. She had somehow counted on it, particularly after a quick survey of the other two couples while Paul was dancing, because the whole group had that moneyed gleam which suggested people with better things to do and posher places to go than an open-air town disco. It was annoying to be aware that they were still there—and to see Ted's eyes wandering past her from time to time with a very thoughtful expression in them. After a while Sara grew tired of deliberately *not* looking round, of getting a crick in her neck keeping her head turned the other way. She moved her chair a little, and let her eyes drift as if casually.

There was nothing casual about the dark eyes fixed on her from the next table, drawing her like a magnet. But, before she could pretend surprise—or coldness, or disdain—the dark, brooding gaze looked right through her without the faintest acknowledgement, and moved away as Paul turned his head to make some pleasant remark to one of his companions.

Somehow after that the evening snowballed. Sara became the life and soul of the party, seized with an uncharacteristic vivacity which set the rest of the group off onto drinking more, dancing more, fooling about with noisy high-spirits. Their table became the noisiest in the place, particularly after Jean-Claude started spiking everyone's drinks with vodka, and at some point Sara found herself holding Ted up to ridicule for trying to make them tone it down a bit: how could he be so stuffy and middle-aged, when he was only a year older than she was? And then she had to kiss him to show she didn't really mean it, particularly when he'd just bought her a shiny Sainte-Vierge-fish pendant from a pedlar who was coming round the tables selling them; and then she had to kiss all the others in case anyone felt left out. She egged everyone on to dance, and when Ted wouldn't, danced by herself, or with Jean-Claude: the thumping beat, the jostling bodies, the bright disco lights blinking on and off, went into a whirl of gaiety. If Sara's head was aching a bit, and she had begun to feel a bit sick, that was nothing, and would soon pass off—particularly now the lights had dimmed to go with a slow number and she had Jean-Claude's convenient shoulder to lean against... She muttered a cross, 'Stop it', as he began to hold her too tightly and one of his hands showed even more than its usual tendency to wander. She knew, dimly, that she hadn't been behaving at all like her usual self, but that was no reason to let him think she planned to be *that* encouraging. And then with a sobering shock she realised that they weren't surrounded by people any more, but right off the dance-floor and round behind one of the canvas barriers; that he had danced her into an empty, dim, secluded corner where there was no-one else around at all.

'Jean-*Claude*! That's enough, behave—'

'*Sara, belle Sara, tu es si belle*—!'

He wasn't showing the least inclination to behave, and the alcohol on his breath as he tried to find her evasive mouth was almost overwhelming. One of his hands was sliding up her bare thigh and as she tried to wriggle away from him she came up against the hardness of a stone wall behind her. Jean-Claude, pinning her there, seemed to think her attempts to push him off were all part of the game and muttered something with a drunken laugh as she tried breathlessly to restrain first one of his hands, then the other, and twist her head away from his seeking lips. He was stronger than he looked and, Sara realised abruptly, totally determined to get exactly what he wanted—and expected...

He was pulled away from her with such extraordinary suddenness that she could scarcely believe it. One moment she was fighting him, the next moment he wasn't there. As she blinked in the filtering light which suddenly seemed very bright, Sara could see *why* he wasn't there. He was sitting in an ungainly heap on the pavement three feet away with his mouth gaping open in almost comical surprise. There was nothing funny about the expression of the man who stood over him for a second, and then stepped back to turn the same icy, scornful, murderous look on Sara.

'Are you sober enough to walk?' he asked coldly, with a crackle of anger in his voice which somehow did nothing to detract from the cool, amazingly unruffled elegance of his appearance. 'Because if so—'

'*Paul, look out—*'

It was seeing Jean-Claude move which made her find her voice with such urgency; seeing him rise into a dangerous crouch, with the flash of steel in one hand which sent the whole thing into a nightmare. The boy was swaying a little, but his dark, street-wise eyes were as murderous as the man's had been a second ago. Sara wanted to shout, 'Jean-Claude, don't be such a fool,' but her tongue had frozen: the whole scene seemed to have frozen as the tall man and the crouching boy faced each other for the space of an indrawn breath. Then, with a suddenness which made it seem totally unreal, a third figure was amongst them, and with a remarkably rapid grasp of the situation, had broken the spell.

It was Elli. She spat something at Jean-Claude in an accent Sara couldn't understand, and brought a hand down on his wrist at the same moment in a chopping motion which suggested she was all too familiar with street fights. The knife clattered from his fingers and bounced away across the stone, helped by a swift sweeping kick from Elli's foot to send it thoroughly out of range, while she dragged

Jean-Claude to his feet with one strong arm and began to pull him away. In spite of the practicality of her behaviour her face was white and frightened as she turned it towards Paul and her voice, even while she was retreating, had a plea in it.

'He wouldn't have done any harm, m'sieur, honestly, he's very drunk that's all, you don't have to call the cops—'

They were gone, with Elli dragging Jean-Claude into a stumbling run which took him out of range and out of sight. Sara found her breath quavering out on a sob, and was suddenly glad of the wall behind her holding her up. Paul hadn't moved—and as he turned his head now to look at Sara she was suddenly and horribly aware of her dishevelled appearance and, even more soberingly, that he had just rescued her from a near-rape, which, he must be as aware as she was, had been to a great extent her own fault.

'You have an odd choice of friends,' he said coldly. 'Or do you prefer Marseilles riff-raff?'

'No...I mean...You're *not* going to call the police, are you?'

'It would be just about what you deserve, for getting publicly drunk and making an exhibition of yourself—but no, I shan't. These things tend to happen at festivals.' The comment was short and unfriendly, and Sara felt miserably sure that the anger in his voice was more for her than for Jean-Claude. He walked abruptly away from her and bent down to retrieve the knife, weighing it in his hand for a moment and then closing it and putting it in his pocket, and speaking to her over his shoulder. 'Tidy yourself up, for goodness sake. And then I'll take you home.'

'No, you don't have to, I can go with the others—' She was already pulling her dress back into place with hasty fingers, and trying to do something with her hair too, though it was falling down to the extent where the only thing to do was to take the pins out altogether. She rubbed a hand across her mouth and hoped the lighting was dim enough to hide the scarlet in her cheeks—though it was bright enough for her to catch the disbelief in Paul's expression as his head jerked round towards her. 'I—I wasn't just with *him*,' she said hastily, 'someone else is driving, you really don't have to bother! And I'm *not* drunk,' she added crossly—feeling, just at that moment, stone cold sober apart from a slightly wobbly feeling in her legs.

The wobbly feeling grew worse as Paul stepped sharply towards her. 'I said,' he told her softly, but with menace in it, 'I will take you home. Unless of course you want to finish that scene I interrupted—'

'Don't you dare sneer at me! You know perfectly well—' Sara choked, because for no good reason tears were clogging her voice, and they were tears which had something to do with the fact that he was standing so close to her but looking at her with anger and scorn. 'You wouldn't even bother to admit you knew me, earlier,' she said, without meaning to say that at all, and staring up at him resentfully. 'I wasn't good enough for you to say hello to then, so you can leave me alone now—'

'You really have drunk too much, haven't you? I wonder what's going to come out next?'

'Nothing, except that I wish you'd go away!'

'Yes, you made *that* clear enough yourself,

earlier on. All the same you're going to come down to the car with me now—'

'I'm not!'

'Yes, you are, if I have to drag you there.' His hand closed round her wrist, and tightened as she instinctively twisted away: the warm strength of his fingers somehow made her want to cry all over again. 'God knows why I feel that you shouldn't be left running around loose, in the circumstances, but for some illogical reason I do. So you'll *go* where you're told, and *do* what you're told—'

The anger in his voice had somehow changed, so that the air between them was charged with something else—something which made Sara sway towards him instead of pulling away, her eyes which had been fixed defiantly on his were suddenly held there by the dark magic of his nearness. She was scarcely aware that the disco music had stopped and the silence made her ears hum, or that faint crackles and bangs had started somewhere in the distance. And then, abruptly, there was the clear sound of a woman's voice somewhere near at hand, calling out with a faintly

186

querulous note,

'Paul? Paul, *chéri*, where on earth have you got to—?'

Sara was sharply aware of Paul's hand dropping her wrist, as he stepped away from her almost with the air of a man who had suddenly woken up. As the tall, elegant blonde who had been with him all evening came round the end of the canvas barrier and saw him she began reproachfully, 'The fireworks are starting, darling, and we're all waiting to go—'

'Yes, I'm sorry. There's an employee I have to take home, unfortunately, as she's rather too tight to look after herself—can you go with the others?'

Sara didn't know why she had forgotten his blonde, but she had, totally. Nothing could have stung her into sharper remembrance than the bored note in Paul's voice. She moved quickly out from behind him on legs which were almost steady, and made sure her voice *was* steady as she said with a sweet meekness she was far from feeling, 'It's quite all right, Monsieur Merinard, honestly, my boyfriend'll get me home all right, don't worry. Goodnight, madame!'

She walked past both of them, feeling viciously glad when the woman gave her a sharp and slightly suspicious look for the steadiness of her progress: if Paul's lady-friend cared to assume the obvious, that should cause a nice little disagreement later. He made no further attempt to stop Sara's departure and it was only a couple of seconds later anyway, when she ran slap into Ted, who seized her by the arm and started hustling her along for all the world, she thought crossly, as if she really *was* his girlfriend and he was annoyed at having mislaid her—and where had *he* been when she needed him, anyway? She was opening her mouth to ask him that, and to ask him not to walk so fast because it was making her dizzy again, when she realised he was talking urgently to her as they went.

'Ellie's taken Jean-Claude down to the van, she said she'll sit on him if necessary to keep him there. Come on, we're all going to leave pronto—God, Sara, you really do cause trouble—'

'I don't, that's not fair!'

'He isn't going to call the police, is he? That bloke you "don't know"? Anyway we'd better get Jean-Claude out of here fast, just in case! Oh, for goodness sake, don't start *crying*—I know you're tight, but you did ask for...whatever it was you got, and as far as I can gather it wasn't much, through no fault of yours! I should have guessed you couldn't look after yourself,' he said gloomily as he dragged Sara along with him, 'but it's bad enough being responsible for the camp lot, without you as well. Come on, we left the van by the station, it's *this* way!'

She wanted to protest, and to tell him that he ought to stop behaving like everybody's uncle too, but somehow being walked along so fast was making her feel a lot less sober than she thought she was and she had to concentrate on staying upright and in one piece. She went on concentrating until they were in the van and then she must have fallen into a sudden sleep because the next thing she was properly aware of was being walked up the hill by Ted, with the night air cool on her face and the stars very bright above, and knowing

189

from the shapes around them that they were back on the caravan site. He had an arm round her which felt companionable, even though it was probably only there to prop her up—which wasn't really necessary any more, because although she was still feeling a little fuzzy round the edges her legs were working again. More than anything she was aware of feeling deeply, resentfully unhappy and that it seemed to have a lot to do with life being unfair. And inexplicable. And there was obviously something wrong with *her* which made life come out so unfairly. When they reached the caravan she leaned against the side of it while Ted fumbled in his pocket for the master-key, muttering that she *was* awake, thanks, and quite capable of standing up on her own if she wanted to.

'Didn't you *know* that watering your wine'd make you drunk quicker?' Ted asked on a note of sorely-tried patience. 'Let alone—'

'Hush, you'll wake Ruth,' Sara retorted, seizing on the first excuse she could think of; and heard his dark shape beside her give an exasperated sigh.

'Don't be silly. Yes, I *know* she's supposed to sleep on the site and that I'm not supposed to know that she doesn't, but I'm not thick! Sometimes I wonder why I ever took this job,' he muttered, crossly enough for Sara to realise that he was having a remarkable amount of trouble with the key. 'Sometimes I really do wonder if it wasn't better being a redundant graduate on the dole instead of being expected to police over-sexed teenagers and cope with lovesick—Damn!'

'Ted?'

'Yes, what?'

'What *is* it about me? I mean, seriously?' She wasn't feeling drunk any more, but the alcohol she had consumed had loosened her tongue enough for her to put the question into words, here in the dark. 'Why don't I *ever* land up with someone nice like you, instead of—'

'For God's sake, Sara—'

'No, I'm not making a pass at you, honestly! I just want to know! I'm asking you as a *friend*, see?' She frowned, trying to put it clearly, because in her present dispirited state. It seemed important to find an answer. 'I suppose I'm reasonably pretty, at least people say so. But the *nice* ones don't ever ask me out. Let alone the fact that—that whenever *I* fall for someone it's always the wrong person, I don't ever get to *know* the other kind! There must be something about me which puts them off, and I wish you'd tell me what it is!'

'Well, I'll be—' she heard him give something between a sigh and a laugh. 'You really *don't* know, do you? All right then—since I'm not *entirely* sober myself, I'll try and give you a lesson on how men's minds work! It's because you're a lot more than "reasonably pretty," for a start—'

'I'm not!'

'Shut up and listen. You're beautiful—like something out of a dream. Now, it takes a bloke with a lot of confidence to walk up to someone beautiful and ask for a date. For one thing, he'll imagine that she's got lots of men standing in line already. For another, he'll think, what have *I* got to offer someone like that? She'd just look at me and laugh. Then again, with you,' he went on thoughtfully, 'when you're not going crazy like you were tonight, for your own reasons—you've got a funny sort of detachment about you. As if you were living somewhere else, in a world of your own—'

'That's only because I work on my own a lot! And—well, sometimes it's because I used to be shy, and shy people use that as a defence! Also I—I was brought up in rather an unusual way, I suppose, with everyone doing their own thing a lot—'

'Yes, I was going to say, I bet you didn't grow up with a lot of other children around. Ha, I haven't got a psychology degree for nothing,' Ted said, sounding owlish. 'Well, there's your answer, if you wanted one. It's the way you look. And now, for safety's sake, I think we'd both better go our own ways and sleep it off—'

'It's not fair, though, is it?'

'Sara,' Ted said with an explosive note in his voice. 'Will you please go inside that damned caravan now I've got it unlocked for you, and stop making me feel inclined to comfort you?'

'Oh—yes—sorry—'

193

'Goodnight,' he said firmly as she pulled the door open. He was, she thought, particularly careful not to touch her as she climbed up into the caravan, and she was just as careful not to hesitate and smile at him as she shut the door behind her. She liked Ted very much—but she didn't want to make her feelings all the more confused by spending the night with him. She was well aware, as she plumped down on to her bunk, that the misery still there inside her came from knowing that she'd been standing under the stars with the wrong man...and that it would have felt quite different under that bright, glittering arch of beauty with the *right* man. It didn't help at all to find herself wishing wistfully that it could have been the right man telling her she was 'beautiful—like something out of a dream'— and that he would say it lovingly, instead of with a mocking, sardonic note in his voice.

It made it even worse to know that while *she* could drift into that fantasy, *he* was un- doubtedly using all his loving words on some- one else.

CHAPTER SEVEN

A thumping headache didn't help her to feel like work. It didn't seem just, either, that she could be hung-over but still remember last night so clearly: if she had been *that* drunk it ought to have gone into a blur. Instead she could remember only too well how bored Paul had sounded about thinking he ought to take her home. She set her teeth on edge making herself visualise his lady-friend in detail: tall, soignée, not beautiful but striking, perhaps a little dark-skinned against the smoothly-sculptured short blonde hair, but with those dramatic eyes as dark as Paul's own. Expensive-looking, with an air of cool sophistication and very long, very elegant legs. A particular type, obviously *his* type, a fact which Sara would do well to remember, she thought bad-temperedly.

If she tried hard enough she might be able to convince herself she was only bad-tempered because of the headache—which certainly wasn't helped by the sun shining brightly in from the villa garden: for once she could almost have done with Marie's desire to close the shutters. Not that Marie was making any complaints about that nowadays, in fact she had just demonstrated a continuing urge to be helpful by coming in silently with an un-solicited cup of coffee. The coffee was so weak and tasteless that Sara could be sure (with a touch of self-mockery) that it didn't have weed-killer in it; and when she had thought of that, she had to restrain herself from thinking with unaccustomed bitterness that she wouldn't care if it *had*. She told herself quickly not to be stupid. She wasn't the only person in the world with a hangover—and she kept her mind firm-ly on that—because Louis, Francine, and even Ted had shown signs of wincing at any sud-den noise this morning, while Jean-Claude wasn't visible at all. Sara had felt a little awkward when she ran into Elli, only to find the other girl giving her a cheerful grin without any sign of grudge. Elli, who obviously had a philosophical nature, jerked her thumb in the direction of Jean-Claude's living quarters, and said blithely, 'Whew, eh? That'll teach him to keep his head down in future!'

Sara let out a sigh, and tried to concentrate on the work she had set herself for this afternoon. It wasn't at all useful to find herself wondering, suddenly, why on earth she was still doing this job. It was a contract, she had to stick to it. She *wanted* to stick to it, and if her stubbornness suddenly seemed to have holes in it, she must remember that it was a matter of principle to stick to things. In fact the notes she was trying to type out were really quite interesting, and no doubt shortly she would go back to finding them so. It was an account of the closing up of the Lorivel factory during war-time because the Merinard then in charge had refused to do any work at all for an occupying power, and Sara had found it fascinating to begin with, piecing the story together from old newspaper clippings and notes Mr Halberson had started to make on odd pieces of paper and the backs of envelopes. She had decided to type it up because it *was* in such random scraps, some of them on clippings which were falling to pieces from age, and because 'The Occupation' would obviously be a small but relevant piece of history for Lorivel; and it was only a pity that she couldn't seem to find it so absorbing today. Only because of her headache, of course.

She glanced out again at the sunlight, crossly, and decided that she might let herself off at half-past four and go and swim, to see if that would help: the sea was beginning to warm up now, particularly in the late afternoons. And she really must find Monsieur Julien sometime and see if she *could* manage to question him: the Second World War probably wouldn't seem such a long time ago to him, something he actually remembered rather than old history. She wondered if it was one of his days today, frowning a little because she had the impression someone had actually walked past the window a moment ago.

She didn't look up when the study door opened, because she was in the middle of deciphering some words on a crease on a newspaper clipping, but kept her finger and her eyes on the place and used her other hand to push the empty coffee cup towards the edge of the desk so that Marie could take it away, murmuring a polite thanks. The hand which came into the edge of her vision instead of Marie's made her stiffen into awareness as it moved the cup deliberately to one side and placed a shiny, tinselly pendant on the desk beside her. Sara felt her heart give one thump, and then an odd coldness took over. She turned her head a little, as if casually, but without raising her eyes, and heard her own voice say coolly.

'If you wouldn't mind waiting one moment, Monsieur Merinard, while I just finish this, I'll be with you in a moment.'

He waited in silence while she went back to the newspaper, studied it, turned to her typewriter and typed a word. Then at last she looked up. She had expected to find him studying her, and had schooled her expression into a cool politeness—but he was looking round the room with a slight frown. There was a touch of surprise in it, which gave her the advantage: she had almost forgotten that he hadn't seen the room since she cleaned it. She was grimly certain that she was going to seize every advantage she could, and said pointedly,

'I'm a great deal more organised now, as you can see. The room was far too dirty to work in properly, but I can assure you, I haven't thrown anything away. Everything's in those boxes, which I'm gradually sorting into files. Perhaps you'd care to see some of them?'

'I'm rather surprised to find you working today,' he said drily, looking at her. Studying her, Sara thought, to see if she would blush. She wasn't in a blushing mood. She looked back at him steadily, keeping her eyes on his and managing to feel nothing at all but a cold hostility.

'Oh?' she said politely. 'But you happened to be passing?'

'I came to make sure that you'd got back safely—naturally.'

'As you can see, m'sieur.'

'How very formal, Miss Farrow!' Her control must be annoying him, because a muscle jumped in his cheek when she managed to give him a look of polite surprise. 'I also came to give you *that*—which I presume must be yours, since I found it on the ground after you'd left.' His eyes indicated the Sainte-Vierge pendant which Sara had been carefully ignoring. 'Only a fairground trifle, I know—but it might have had some sentimental value for you!'

'Then how kind of you to bring it back,' Sara said with sweet indifference. 'Would you like to see some of my work now? This one is...let me see, letters written in Indian. At least I suppose it's an Indian language, since I know your great-uncle lived there. You'll probably want to have them translated, though they may be merely personal. And this one's—'

'Yes, I can see that you've been working hard.' He sounded impatient, and Sara took care to keep her attention on the files she was drawing out of their pile. 'You're obviously very capable. I'm not a slave-driver, however, and it *is* Saturday. I didn't mean you to feel that you had to work all hours—'

'I don't. When I work on a Saturday I take another day off during the week instead. I'm keeping an accurate record of hours worked,' Sara said with cool formality, 'which I can send to your secretary, if you'd like. This week and...let's see, next week's, are up on the wall over there. Perhaps you'd like to look at them now and tell me if they're satisfactory. Oh, and—'

'Why do I get the distinct feeling I'm being put in my place? Do you know,' he said deliberately as she turned to look up at him, 'I would have thought I deserved thanks, in the circumstances—wouldn't you?'

'If you think you deserve thanks for reminding me of an embarrassing situation, and for making so much out of it, then thank you. What I was about to say,' Sara told him, making an almost inhuman effort to keep her voice calm instead of snapping the words at him— and discovering suddenly that her headache had gone, presumably pushed away by the rush of adrenalin caused by losing her temper with him—'was that—that I presume if I finish the work ahead of time, the contract comes to an end? You only wanted the papers sorting, after all—'

'Shall we have a truce, Sara?'

The words were totally unexpected. So was the rueful note in his voice, and the smile which had come into his eyes. It made him look so human—and so charming—that Sara almost blinked. It was almost impossible to resist smiling back at him: unfortunately it was just as irresistible to feel a swift suspicion that he knew that. Sara swallowed hard, and wished she could manage to look at him without feeling weak with longing. She found herself saying, uncertainly,

'Are we at war, then?'

'It's been a bit like that, hasn't it? I think you know what I mean.' The smile was still there, even if it had a swift sardonic twist to it. 'I'm still not quite sure, but...maybe we could change the rules a bit. Have dinner with me tonight.'

'Why?'

The word came out bluntly, when all she wanted to say was yes. His eyes narrowed a little, but he seemed prepared to give the question proper consideration.

'Shall we say, because you were quite right

to call me ill-mannered for reminding you of an embarrassing situation? Or would you rather I said, because you draw me against my will?'

'That—doesn't sound like a very good reason—'

'All right then. Let's say it occurs to me that you've been very isolated here. I've been busy and left you to it, when I should have seen that you had—shall we say, more suitable company? You've worked hard: this room shows that. Perhaps I feel that you deserve an outing.' A muscle was jumping in his jaw again, and Sara knew, suddenly, that he wasn't used to being turned down. Or even questioned. And what he was saying, now, was unmistakeable: she'd been left on her own too much so it wasn't surprising she'd got into bad company. And, in his casual, lordly way, he felt responsible. She remembered again with a sudden sick clarity that bored note in his voice last night, and an angry shame swept through her that she'd wanted so much to accept his charitable offer. Or perhaps it wasn't so charitable: perhaps, well away from his smooth friends with whom he could talk and laugh like an ordinary human being, he wanted Sara as an entertainment, someone to play with! She looked up at him with an anger she tried hard to conceal because it contained too much hurt and resentment, and said very politely,

'Thank you, but I'm already doing something tonight. And you needn't worry about my being alone, because I'm not!'

'Sara—'

He was saying her name with an angry edge to it when the door opened. It opened with an abruptness which was unlike Marie, but it was she who stood there, blinking a little, and with an oddly mottled look to her skin which Sara noticed without being more than half aware of it. Perhaps she had been hurrying, because she spoke in a breathless rush, with her eyes fixed waveringly on Paul.

'Your assistant from Lorivel is telephoning you, m'sieur. I think he's still holding on. You know I'm not very good with the telephone, m'sieur, but I think he wants you to go back there—'

The thick southern French faltered as Paul

stepped past her, saying impatiently, 'Yes, all right, I'll come and speak to him!' As he left, Marie flinched back out of his way—and it was that more than anything which reminded Sara abruptly that she *hadn* told Paul she wasn't sleeping at the villa any more. Nor why. If Marie had listened at the door before opening it she wouldn't know that, because they had been talking in English. An impulse of pity made her call the old woman back. She had behaved like a madwoman, certainly—but perhaps the mounting tension in her had been broken by that, because now she looked like nothing so much as a very old woman who was worried about being sacked without a pension. Sara made the excuse of asking her to remove the coffee cup, and got up as if casually to push the door closed.

'Marie—'

'He was wanted on the telephone, mam'selle, but I'm not very good with it—'

'Yes, I'm sure he understands that. Marie, I haven't found any need to speak to Monsieur Merinard about my not staying here—you understand? It didn't seem necessary to discuss it with him—at the moment,' she added for safety's sake. 'Do you agree?'

'Whatever mam'selle wishes.' She hadn't been too deaf to hear what Sara said—and for a second Sara wondered if she had been wise to say it, because she could almost have sworn a flicker of the old malevolence showed briefly in the housekeeper's eyes. Then the door was pushed open again and Paul was back.

'I'm leaving,' he said curtly, in Sara's direction. His dark eyes rested on her angrily, thoughtfully, though all he said was, with annoyance, 'We were cut off, but I presume I'm wanted. Sara—'

'Lorivel's working on a Saturday too? How very busy you must be!'

'As everyone knows.' There was still anger in the unfathomable glance he gave her, but it broke on a frown as he glanced at Marie, and he said half-absently, though still in English, 'I meant to ask you if everything was all right, is it?'

'Yes,' Sara said, aware of the way the old woman was straining to grasp what was being said in a language she didn't understand.

Suddenly she wanted to change what she had said to Paul, with a craven longing to accept his invitation no matter what the reason for it: just to be with him would be enough. But the situation had changed now and he was too busy to want to see her, so she had lost her chance. And she didn't know what to say to bring him back again; or to change the frown in his eyes to a smile.

He had turned to Marie now, saying clearly but with an odd gentleness, 'Don't try to work too hard: Miss Farrow is very capable of looking after herself. M. Halberson would be very pleased to have his work carried on so well, I think. Will you give my regards to M. Julien and tell him I'll come to see him at his cottage some time soon?' Then, without sparing a further glance for Sara, he was gone. And she was left wishing quite ridiculously that he would speak to *her* with that much gentleness—a thought to be resisted so strongly that she sat down with an angry thump to go on with her work. She wanted to run after him to the car, but made herself sit still and crush the stupid impulse, defending herself with memories. Paul sneering at her, mocking her—it was better to remember him like that than letting herself be betrayed by the memory of those other moments when there had seemed to be a thread of understanding between them, when she had felt that he was a man she could like as well as feeling so dizzyingly, overwhelmingly drawn to him.

She reminded herself bitterly that she had already made a fool of herself once this year, and should be warned. Somehow, though, it was no use trying to conjure up Dennis's fair and handsome face because it merely blurred into a darker, stronger one. The feelings she had known then were nothing but a pale shadow of the ache and longing she felt now. Her convenient escape had achieved nothing more than taking her out of the frying pan into the fire. She told herself with self-mockery that she had just been ready to fall in love, that was all; that she was suffering from a delayed adolescence; that she would have to live through it. She had better cultivate some of the 'detachment' Ted had told her she had—instead of wondering unhappily whether

Paul would stay away this time or come back...

If his face kept coming between her and her work over the next few days—to be rigidly pushed away—he didn't appear in person. Her rigidly self-imposed concentration didn't stop Sara noticing, either, that Marie was beginning to behave oddly again. It was nothing she could pin down, but it gave her a vague feeling of unease. When she found herself thinking that it would give her the perfect excuse to ring up Paul, she decided immediately that she was just imagining things. It *wasn't* because he might turn up, either, that she kept strictly to office hours for her work at the villa and didn't take advantage of the hot, sultry, beginning-of-June weather which as if working to the calendar had begun to burn in earnest as soon as May was over. It was certainly hot enough to bathe in the evenings now, and the beaches were emptier then too as the families with small children began to pack up and go indoors to shower and rest before a long lazy dinner eaten on balconies overlooking the sea or, up on the caravan site, at open-air tables with bright umbrellas.

The tourists were coming in regularly now in weekly or fortnightly batches to stay in the caravans parked up on the hillside in carefully spaced rows—the largest and most expensive ones right at the top with their wide picture-windows facing outwards, because even if it was the most inconvenient place into which to manoeuvre a large caravan up the steep hair-pin bends, it had the best view, a magnificent panorama of sea and coast. Sara had gone up to admire it all, even going up to watch the sunset from there one night and trying not to wish, wistfully, that she wasn't watching the rose and crimson and purple and gold all alone. A bunch of young German students who were camping down below in tents arrived up there too, and began to jostle and show off and whisper with side-long glances in her direction: Sara could have joined them, she knew, by just turning her head. She remembered what Ted had said about her, but she *didn't* turn her head, and went on looking 'detached' until they moved away again. It wasn't much use telling herself to be sensible and get on with her own life when her heart kept telling her she was waiting...waiting on the offchance, and for something so disturbing and dangerous that it would do her no good at all. But even knowing *that* didn't help.

She spent most of her evenings helping on the site, telling herself that it wasn't because she preferred to be busy than to have time to think, but because the work was there to be done. Ted was his normal amiable self, but growing increasingly busy as the tourist season picked up, and new staff had been taken on for the office, campers kept arriving and had to be told where they could pitch tents, and there was an endless job cleaning out fixed caravans after one rental and before the next. If Ted hadn't been so busy, Sara thought as she walked up after her swim one evening, she might have mentioned her worry about Marie to him. Today the old woman had seemed to be in a state of constant movement, because Sara had heard her wandering round the house, opening and closing shutters, muttering to herself. When she had come face to face with Sara in the hall she had flinched, and her skin had seemed to have a greenish tinge—

though that was probably only because of the dusky light. Oh well, perhaps it was only the heat which was affecting her. It was only just under a week since Paul came... Sara sighed sharply and pulled herself together. She would stop worrying about Marie, who couldn't really do anything to her now that the only room she ever went into was the easily-escapable study. She would go and help Ruth clean a caravan instead. And after that, she remembered, she'd offered to help Elli down in the cellar below the bar, because a new load of soft drinks had just come in and they'd all got to be stowed in the right places.

It was very late by the time they finished the cellar job. Sara emerged wearily, blinking at the sight of darkness lit by the flaring sodium lights of the camp's roadway, and realised that she'd been underground for hours shifting crates and stacking Coke bottles. She hoped suddenly that Ruth was still on the site because she hadn't brought her caravan key down with her. A glance at her watch showed her that it was almost eleven, so Ruth probably *would* have left, and a quick search round her jeans pocket showed she really hadn't slipped the key absent-mindedly into one of them. Oh well, perhaps Ruth would have left the door unlocked, because she was often careless: if not she'd have to dig out Ted and borrow the master-key, that's all. She called out a cheerful goodnight to Elli and set off to trudge up the road.

It had been hot work, even in the cool of the cellar, and she shivered a little now as the sweat dried on her bare shoulders, because she had stripped down to a minimal suntop for coolness. She found her mind flying back to Marie suddenly—and told herself quickly not to be silly, because her imaginings must be turning into paranoia if she could have the feeling she was being watched *now*, here on the site, from somewhere amongst the dark shapes of the caravans. It was somehow a comfort as well as a piece of practical luck to see Ted a hundred yards ahead crouched over a drain with a rod in his hand (the plumbing must have gone wrong again) and she gave him a grin and a wave as she turned off the road into the darker strip which led towards her caravan, thinking that she would know where he was if the door did turn out to be locked. And then thinking, with a touch of wistfulness as she glanced up with her light-dazzled eyes to see if the stars were still there in their high and beautiful arch above, that it was a pity after all that she couldn't have settled for Ted. Except that *he* had a girlfriend of his own somewhere else, too. Just like everyone else.

The caravan door wasn't locked after all: Sara pulled it open and climbed up inside, drawing the curtains automatically and then switching on the lights. She sat down on her bunk and kicked off her sandals, tugging at the ribbon which had tied her hair up in a pony-tail to keep it out of the way. At least, she thought wryly, she ought to be physically tired enough to sleep without dreaming... without being haunted by a pair of broad shoulders, a dark olive-skinned face which could smile but more often frowned, a voice which could switch from French to English and back again but whose mocking tones could scrape along her nerves...

The door opened with a suddenness which

shook the whole caravan. It closed again with a slam—and with a click of the lock falling into place which Sara only half-registered, because she was gazing up with shock at the tall, dark, broad shouldered figure which was suddenly right there in front of her, taking up far too much space, diminishing the caravan's size by the sheer force of his presence. Diminishing the air she could breathe, too, because she could only gasp as she gazed up into a pair of furious dark eyes. Paul—here? How? And why—?

'So this is where you are,' he grated. 'And don't try to tell me you're not living here— I've been in once already and seen too much of your property lying around! So that was what you meant when you said you "weren't alone", was it?'

She had thought she had seen him angry before. She realised now that she had never seen him quite so close to losing control completely—not even when he had stood over Jean-Claude: his manner then had been ice-cool by comparison. 'How did you—' she began, and then, 'Yes, I do live here, but—I can explain—'

'Don't bother! Just have a good laugh at my expense instead. I've spent most of the evening looking for you—worrying about you—wondering what the hell could have happened to you—without it ever occurring to me that you were happily shacked up *here*.' His eyes, never leaving her face, seemed to burn a scornful hole through her skin. 'I don't know who it is you're living with—no, don't tell me you're not, with someone else's jeans and leather jacket lying about in the other sleeping compartment, where no doubt he *doesn't spend his nights!—but I imagine it's the one you've just waved at, rather than the one who vanished at the sight of me half-an-hour ago. Or both of them, perhaps?'

'*I'm not*—' Sara caught her lower lip between her teeth to stop it shaking. What did it matter what he thought? She wasn't going to let it matter. She brought out, 'Why were you looking for me?'

'Marie's had a stroke. I came over—to see *you*.' The words were full of scorn and, somehow, self-mockery. 'I must have given her

217

a shock, perhaps, I don't know. She started raving. I remembered you'd said...Anyway her mind was obviously wandering, because she was saying some fairly appalling things...After I'd had her taken to hospital—she was unconscious by that time—I started looking for you. It wasn't,' he said with icy rage, 'until I thought to go and see Monsieur Julien that I had any clue you hadn't been done away with, or locked up, or something—but luckily Monsieur Julien still has his intelligence and his powers of observation. He told me you'd moved over here several weeks ago. *He* was surprised I didn't know about it. And if I'd had the sense to go to him sooner—'

'You wouldn't have needed to feel concerned. Or responsible.' Sara wished her voice wouldn't shake, which was only because he was looking at her with such dislike that it was almost unbearable. She found that she was gripping her hands together tightly to stop *them* shaking too. 'How's Marie now?' she asked rapidly.

'Still deeply unconscious. They told me it wasn't worth enquiring again until morning.'

He gave the answer shortly, staring at her across the tiny room with a smouldering disdain. 'Don't you want to hear the rest of my detective work?' he asked mockingly, a cruel curve to his mouth. 'How I was *still* fool enough to be worried about you, and wonder if you were all right? How I enquired for you at the office down below, and had you paged on the camp tannoy? And then found out which caravan you were in and came up here to look? Stupid of me, wasn't it? And,' he asked explosively, 'where the hell have you been, anyway?'

'Working!'

She saw the disbelief in his eyes. It was no use explaining anything to him. He had made up his mind one way: it was no use imagining, wishing, she could change it. It was no use wishing *anything*. 'It isn't any of your business what I do with my own time,' she burst out, 'and you wouldn't believe it anyway, it's no use telling you *anything*—'

'Isn't it my business, Sara? *Isn't* it?'

He came away from the door in one stride which ate up the yard of floor between them.

219

He was down beside her before she could move, reaching for her like a man goaded beyond endurance. She heard him say, *'Isn't it?'* again, his face still angry, his hands rough as they seized her. There was no tenderness in his touch, no caress in the way his lips came down hard on hers, only passion and fury.

If his kiss was bruising, the arms which pulled her against him were bruising too. His fingers dug into her, making her wince, and then tore the cotton top away to dig into her skin. When his lips moved to her throat, then to her breasts, Sara knew only that the hard demand of his mouth drew all the starving longing inside her to the surface. There was no need for words, no need to beg him never to stop, never to leave her. It didn't matter that he had been angry, because the hard tension in him now was all passion, sweeping both of them. She was gasping with it, caught by the magnetism of him which drew the soul out of her body and replaced it with a wild beating in her blood. He pushed her back on to the bunk, his hands and lips moving over her, the length of him heavy against her so that she twisted against him with a moan. When his mouth came back to hers its hard sweetness seemed to melt her very bones. His hand was fumbling to undo her jeans but she didn't care: there was an inevitability about loving him which made the rest only natural...

She heard him say, harshly, 'If you're anyone's, you can also be mine!'

It caught her like a barb. Suddenly, weakly, she was struggling, and she heard her own voice coming out on a husky, breathless, broken plea.

'Oh please, Paul—not like that, hating me— *please*—'

His only response was to push her back against the bunk, with his hands moving ruthlessly over her.

CHAPTER EIGHT

It was stupid not to want to come out of the
caravan into the morning light. She couldn't
hide in there forever anyway. Sara, who had
been touching her memories gingerly ever
since she woke, tried to tell herself that it was
a morning for looking bright and cheerful
and—capable. And—unmoved? Well, yes if she
could manage it. She'd got to face Paul, after
all.

She had a sort of memory of his leaving the
caravan when she was still half awake, of his
leaning over her gently to say that he would
see her later down at the villa. She had the
memory of him staying with her all night,
sleeping with his arms round her. She had the
memory of his extraordinary, contrary tenderness which made her shift her feet uncomfor-
tably as she stood ready to leave the caravan.

Well, all right, so he'd been *surprised*, she told herself crossly—startled more like—to find out the unexpected. It *was* unexpected to find out that someone was a virgn at twenty-four, she was well aware of that. She could rehearse the idea of telling him that some things were chance rather than morality, except that she hoped he wouldn't refer to it at all...because what she was—had been, until last night—was her own business. Somehow it made her feel faintly foolish, like an oddity, to remember the change in him afterwards. Though at the time...

Some memories weren't for taking out and examining when she was just about to go out and walk down through the site, so Sara pulled the door open firmly and stepped outside. Sunny again, good. And she ought to be wondering how Marie was. She ought to be wondering too, she supposed, whether the old woman's stroke might have been prevented if she'd swallowed her pride and talked to Paul again about her strangeness: it was obviously all tied up together. Paul...she mustn't keep asking herself how he would greet her. She

223

mustn't wonder if he actually realised that she was so unbearably in love with him that—she pulled her thoughts up sharply, and gave a mechanical smile to a passing camper who had wished her a cheerful good morning, realising that she had walked down through most of the site without seeing any of it at all. And, in spite of everything sensible she was trying to say to herself, she was actually feeling light enough to float, happy enough to sing. And not at all hungry for breakfast, so she'd go straight over to the villa.

She saw Paul as she came out to the road, because he was waiting to cross to her just as she arrived to cross to him. She had to stop the ridiculous feeling that her thoughts were winging to him ahead of her, and walked sedately across in a break in the traffic. Reaching him, looking up at him with a smile which she tried to make normal, she found herself wondering with sudden wariness whether there wasn't a tiny touch of embarrassment in the grave way he was watching her—but surely he was too sophisticated to feel that?—and it made her rush into speech.

'How's Marie this morning? Is she any better?'

'Still unconscious. I was just coming across to find you, because I've got to go to the hospital and talk to them about her.' He had one hand in his pocket, and jingled some coins or keys absently, his dark eyes thoughtful on Sara's face. 'I had a conversation with that friend of yours, by the way. The one who manages the site? He stopped me and asked me who I was—which he has a right to do— and when I told him, he gave me an account of what happened three weeks ago. He thought I ought to know.'

'Oh—'

'He felt he ought to explain why he'd lodged you with the cleaning girls. He gave me a very—pithy account of the danger you'd been in. He obviously thought I ought to have been told about it. And so I should. My fault that you didn't feel able to tell me. All the same—it was silly of you not to, Sara!'

He gave her a smile with that, to take the sting out of it. It was a smile which made her heart turn over. A moment later he was grave again: after a tiny pause in which she knew she ought to be saying all sorts of things, but couldn't find the right words for any of them, he said abruptly.

'You won't be staying there any more, anyway. While I'm gone I want you to pack up everything—all your boxes of papers too—and have them ready to move. All right?'

'Where—'

'I'm going to take you to my grandmother's house. You can't work *here* any more, and I'm going to get the villa closed up. Monsieur Julien can act as caretaker-watchman around the grounds. With a little help from his nephew. You can live *and* work at my grandmother's there's plenty of room. I really have got to go now, I'm afraid,' he went on as Sara opened her mouth, 'I told the hospital I'd be along straight away. We can talk about...all sorts of things, later.'

'When—when will you be back?' she asked, trying to sound practical.

'I'm not sure—an hour? Maybe a little longer. I'll pick you up at the villa.'

To her surprise, while his voice had been

quite unemotional, one hand came out to touch her lightly on the cheek, the briefest of caresses. Perhaps it even surprised him, too, to find himself doing it, because a rueful gleam came into his eye. 'Before I go, just tell me one thing—'

'What?' she asked with sudden defensiveness—and heard him give a little sigh, so that she felt more defensive than ever. But the question when it came was so far from anything she might have expected that it left her staring.

'Where exactly *were* you in those two days between leaving London and coming down here?'

'Where *was* I? I was in Paris!'

'Doing...?'

'Wandering about, mostly! I did grow up there, you know! And—I went and put flowers on my grandfather's grave, of course, which was what I stopped off in Paris for in the first place. It occurred to me that I hadn't done that for ages and that if I was coming to Paris it'd be a good chance—why?'

'Never mind.' The rueful gleam was even

more pronounced, and he shook his head, almost as if it was the only way to clear it of cobwebs. 'Yes, I believe you! You *would* want to do that, wouldn't you? Perhaps I'll explain some time how much it confused me—or perhaps I won't, in case it makes you too angry! Go and pack, little one!'

There was a caress in the words—and he had called her 'little one' last night, too, in French; so that the memory of that must surely have brought her heart into her eyes. She was sure he saw it as he turned away to walk to his car parked a few yards down the road, because there was an answering gentleness in the look he gave her. She knew she mustn't stand staring after him with a silly grin on her face because he had made it clear that there were practical matters to be handled which took precedence over everything else; but the smile was there like a Cheshire cat's as she went into the villa to start packing up. She probably *shouldn't* be feeling so fizzy and light-hearted when there was poor old Marie to be thought of with suitable gravity—and when there were all sorts of sensible, reasonable doubts she ought to be making herself dwell on. All the same she didn't want to dwell on them and the smile kept breaking through all the time she was heaping all her carefully-organised files back into the cardboard boxes and carrying them out to make a gradually increasing pile in the hall. It was one thing to remind herself that very little had actually been said in words last night: it was another to remember a combination of passion and tenderness which could very easily be mistaken for love...

She was ready within the specified hour, and had fetched her luggage over from the site too. Saying goodbye to Ted had held a touch of awkwardness because he had given her a funny, resigned look which almost held a touch of, 'I hope you know what you're getting into,' though all he actually said was, 'You know where to find me if you need me, okay?' Then she had gone back to the villa to wait for Paul. If it seemed a long wait, sitting on the doorstep in the sun, she didn't mind. There was a remarkable contentment in waiting for him—though she did find herself wondering a little why he was choosing to take her to his grandmother.

She had left the gates open so that he could drive in. When the sound of a car brought her to her feet, it was with a sharp longing simply to *see* him; so it was a disappointment to find herself looking at a stranger at the wheel of a large station-wagon. He was an efficient-looking young man in shirtsleeves who leapt out and gave her a half-salute, saying,

'Car from Lorivel to take you and a lot of luggage up to the manor, mams'elle. Just show me where it is and I'll load it. Monsieur Paul asked me to say that he's been held up at the hospital, so I'm to take you up instead. Oh, and he says, will we see all the shutters are closed and the place locked up.'

'Yes, I've done that.' It had seemed practical, and she had cleared up in the kitchen too, feeling a certain pathos at the sight of a few dishes in the sink and Marie's familiar overall hanging on the back of a chair. There was only the front door to lock and that was soon done after the efficient young man had loaded all the boxes and Sara's suitcases into the back of the station-wagon, refusing her offer of help and moving to and fro with economical ease. She was still swallowing her disappointment at not seeing Paul, but climbed into the car beside the driver without questioning it because if he had been held up at the hospital, then he had. It didn't seem worth asking the silent if cheerful driver how Marie was, because if he'd come down from Lorivel he'd hardly know. However, a few moments later when they stopped briefly in Boulouris to drop her key off at Monsieur Julien's cottage, she learned that her driver was actually the old gardener's grandson, so put the question as he came back and re-started the car.

'Do you know how the old lady is—?'

'Madame Pelle? Died without coming round, 'bout half an hour ago. Better, I should think—she's been lost without old m'sieur to fuss over. Anyway she's been getting steadily battier for years,' he said cheerfully, and then lapsed back into silence as he swung round behind St Raphael to take the quickest route inland.

Sara hadn't got as far as wondering where Paul's grandmother lived, and didn't like to ask as they switched onto the autoroute and sped northwards. Somewhere near Grasse, since they went on northwards through ground which grew abruptly hillier. The driver seemed inclined to stick to main roads and she realised that they had twisted back when she saw a signpost leading off to Mandelieu; and then Cannes; and a moment later she realised that they must now be on the same road she had travelled before in the coach on her day-trip. The plains and fields of the flower-growing country began to spread out around them; and it occurred to her with sudden regret that if she was going to be working in-land from now on, she would miss the sea. On the other hand it really was beautiful here—and she remembered Paul's saying that he preferred the mountains. The climbing road took them up again, through woods which closed too tightly round the road to allow a view, with Grasse itself somewhere ahead, and she began to wonder if Paul's grandmother lived in Grasse itself. However the driver turned sharply as soon as he reached its out-skirts, apparently knowing his way to 'the manor' without hesitation, and swept on through twisty lanes which suddenly opened out into much higher mountains than before. Perhaps not true mountains but high enough, looming suddenly in forested peaks with grey slashes of rock and scree and patches of purple heather to catch the sun, wild and dramatic. The mountains were still there on their right as they slowed for a village marked St Jean de Peylou, small but cheerful-looking and with a far-from-rural supermarket displaying its plate-glass modernity in the middle of it; and just as they were coming out of the other end of the village the driver slowed still further, hooted, and turned into a drive. It would seem they had arrived.

It was a typical French manor, Sara could see as they approached up a straight drive through an over-formal and carefully-tended garden: built foursquare out of stone with a steep curly-edged roof to give it the look of a castle. Her first impression, dauntingly, was that it was very large and had almost the air of a stately home, but as they came closer she saw that it was elegantly-proportioned rather than big, and probably had no more than six bedrooms. She wished all over again that Paul was with her, and for quite a different reason, because it suddenly seemed an imposition to be dumped on his grandmother without warning and to arrive by herself with a lot of jumbled luggage. She didn't even know *which* grandmother and what to address her by, and wished suddenly that she had the family tree to hand which might help—but they had stopped by the front door now, and the driver had already leapt out to go and ring the bell. Sara got slowly out of the car, looking round at the carefully-gravelled drive, the regimented rose-bushes just coming into bloom, the overlooking mountains. Somehow she almost expected to see the opening door reveal a butler in full uniform.

Actually it revealed a figure whose familiarity sent her heart down to her stomach with a thump of shock. There was no possibility of her not recognising the woman who stood there with smoothly-sculpted short blonde hair lying close against her head, looking at the new arrivals out of fine, dark, slanted eyes; no possibility at all that it could be anybody else, even if she was differently dressed in well-cut slacks and a blouse. Sara scarcely heard the driver saying in practical tones that he had brought mams'elle up from the Villa Robinet as instructed, and where would madame like him to unload the luggage? She was aware of a whirling, uncomfortable confusion which told her that she was in the wrong place— perhaps they had *come* to the wrong place? Or perhaps the woman in the doorway was just visiting? Yes, that must be it, because Paul *wouldn't* in the circumstances have meant to bring her face to face with someone who—

'You'd better put everything in the hall for the time being,' a light voice was saying. Sara was aware of meeting a pair of eyes which took in her startled gaze with a slight lift of the eyebrow and a touch of amused disdain. 'Ah, the employee again. I'm so sorry, I don't know your name, but please come in! We *are* expecting you!'

'I—thought this was—Monsieur Merinard's grandmother's house?'

'Yes, it does belong to grandmère Chantal,

but Paul and I live here too. Now then, I've got to find a room for you—one to sleep in and one to work in, Paul said—'

'Madame—?' Sara said hesitantly. Somehow she was already in the hall, a place of square polished elegance with doors leading off it and stairs leading away upwards.

'You'd better call me Mylène, I should think. There's no need for us to be too formal if you're going to be living here. Now, let me see, where shall I put you? The room next to grandmère, I think—but please come up quietly because she's resting this morning...and won't be down until after luncheon. As for working...the old study next to the dining-room will do, nobody uses that any more.'

She had put a hand to her cheek while she thought about it. As if in a dream, Sara saw the wedding-ring, with a diamond engagement ring above it. 'Paul and I live here too...'
Paul's wife?

She found she was following Mylène numbly up the stairs. Underneath the numbness, she didn't know what she felt—confusion?

Hurt? Anger? It was better to stick with anger. No wonder Paul had given her that look of faint embarrassment this morning. No wonder he had dropped her wrist so sharply when Mylène came into view at the festival. She wondered bitterly whether the object in bringing her here now, which seemed like cruelty, was to administer an immediate warning rather than make explanations. Or perhaps he thought she knew...It was useless to protest inside herself that there hadn't been a wife marked for him on the family tree. He'd told her he was engaged five years ago to the girl Ysabel, but five years was a long time, and there was no reason why he shouldn't have got married since. Mr Halberson just hadn't updated his chart, that's all.

She found herself going through the motions of being grateful to be here. The bedroom she was shown into, a pleasant, anonymous, chintz-furnished guest-room, looked out over more formal gardens at the back of the house. Mylène insisted on staying with her while she unpacked. She displayed a charming friendliness and perhaps that light, disdainful note in her voice was just her normal way of speaking. What exactly had Sara been doing down at the Villa Robinet? Hadn't she found it a dreadfully gloomy place to work? Leaning against the windowsill in a pose which displayed the tall slenderness of her figure to best advantage, she didn't seem surprised by Sara's subdued manner, perhaps putting it down to the shock of Marie's death. She couldn't know that Sara was gritting her teeth to answer her normally—particularly when it occurred to her, with a sick feeling, that for all she knew, Paul might be arrogant enough to think it was convenient to have a wife and a mistress in the same house... Though he could certainly think again about *that*. Anger sparked sharply to help hide the knot of misery inside her and the knowledge of her own too-innocent foolishness.

'You haven't many things, have you?' Mylène asked pityingly, as Sara hung the last of her clothes in the wardrobe, allowing herself to think with rigid control that she would soon be taking them out again, and packing them all up again. She didn't really know why she was unpacking at all except that it was expected of her—but once she saw Paul, she knew that she would tell him with as much cool casualness as she could muster that she really had decided to quit the job now. *Now.*

'I came by air, madame—Mylène. And I haven't needed much.'

'No, I suppose not. *That's* quite pretty, I suppose, of its type,' Mylène said disdainfully as Sara hung up the only semi-formal dress she had brought with her, which she had slipped in at the last minute in case there had been any evening occasion when she might be expected to dress up. She had an abruptly bitter recollection of the expectations she had had about this job: the pretty, chiffony, strap-topped garment Mylène had indicated suddenly seemed to sum them all up and bring a memory of the cheerful and excited discussions she and Bet had had back in the flat in London. *Put it down to experience,* she jeered at herself with an uncharacteristically sharp cynicism; and found herself interrupting some further comment Mylène was making to ask in a voice perhaps a little too cold for politeness if she could be shown the study now, so that she could put everything away tidily. The words 'before Paul comes back' were unspoken.

It was early afternoon before he came back—a dreaming, buzzing, hot afternoon visible in the garden outside, with the house bathed in quietness and the grandmother still invisible. Sara had taken refuge in the study which was supposed to become her workplace, and had stayed there, on the excuse of needing to put things in order. She had asked politely if she could just have a glass of milk and an apple for luncheon to be eaten at her desk—because she couldn't face the thought of sitting across the table from Mylène Merinard and making conversation, with the likelihood that Paul might walk in at any moment—and she hadn't even managed to get through the apple. It was no use trying to think, because her thoughts were too muddled to be useful, and seemed to include the idea that it was no use hating him, he was as he was, she had walked slap into it out of her own foolishness. She hadn't heard him arrive when the door opened and he walked in, because this study was tucked away off another room at the back of the house. He was just suddenly *there*.

And smiling at her. Her heart did its betraying somersault, even while she tried to stiffen herself into that comfortable feeling of anger, and she couldn't help an idiotic impulse to notice that he looked as if he had had a trying morning and was relieved to be home. He said,

'I'm sorry I couldn't bring you up myself after all, but I see Damien got you here all right. You do seem to be a glutton for work: have you started already?'

'About that—' His casualness had the satisfying effect of bringing her anger sparkling to the surface. 'I've stowed everything, but you can find someone else to sort the rest of the papers. I don't really need to give notice to leave, do I?'

'You don't want to work here?'

'*Should* I?'

He gave her a thoughtful, gentle look which wasn't at all what she was expecting, and which took in her heightened colour and the stiffness with which she was sitting. 'You've decided to be unforgiving?' he asked, with a lift of the eyebrow which was rueful rather than mocking. 'But I shan't *let* you leave, Sara—surely you know that?'

'You can't stop—'

'Can't I? Not even if I ask you nicely? Yes, I know it'll be the first time I've asked you nicely instead of telling you, but even so...'

A tap on the door made him break off with a frown. He was leaning against it, so that he had to move as it opened—to reveal Mylène standing there with a look of pretty hesitation on her face. 'I'm sorry, I expect you're discussing Sara's duties,' she said with a speaking look at Paul out of those dark slanted eyes, 'but you know how grandmère is when she wants something. She's downstairs now and she wants to meet Sara. So could she come along—?'

'All right, I'll bring her in a moment. Go and tell her we're coming.'

There was a touch of impatience in his voice, and somehow that made Sara angrier than ever as Mylène moved away obediently and Paul closed the door quite deliberately behind her. He began, with the same coaxing note he had been using before they were interrupted, 'As I was saying—' but Sara was already getting to her feet.

'I don't think we've got anything further to talk about, you should do as your wife suggests!'

She had been carefully looking away from him, so she sensed rather than saw a stiffness about him. As she glanced round, she saw that his eyes had gone blank—with surprise? There was a touch of anger in them perhaps, though there was none in the light, slightly sardonic voice in which he spoke.

'Mylène isn't my wife, she's my cousin. Do you know, I didn't realise you thought so badly of me, Sara? Yes, perhaps we *haven't* got anything further to talk about, for the moment. Now you must come and meet my grandmother, who doesn't like to be kept waiting, as I expect you gathered. She's eighty years old but in *very* full possession of her faculties—my father's mother, did I explain that?—and I should warn you, she expects a certain formality.'

'Paul—'

'Come along,' he said coolly. 'This *is* still her house, and she's waiting to welcome you into it!'

His expression didn't encourage argument. He opened the door for her, and didn't touch her as she walked past him. Sara—whose heart had lifted abruptly, only to sink again at the impersonal look he was now giving her— walked ahead of him through the dining-room with the feeling that her life had been turned upside-down too many times during the last twenty-four hours. And nothing else could matter as much as that she'd misjudged him so badly.

The grandmother was enthroned—there was no other word for it—in a spacious drawing room. She was tiny, with white hair carefully dressed high on her head, diamonds sparkling on her fingers, and the erect carriage of her generation which brought echoes of a world where *ladies* were quite a different breed from women and acted accordingly. As fine-boned as a small, elegant bird, she had the very dark eyes Paul had inherited, with a slant to them which was noticeably the same as

Mylène's standing beside her. If only she'd seen her before, Sara thought despairingly, she might have had some clue. But she was watching Sara's approach with interest and, surprisingly, with a tiny nod of approval. It was all Sara could do not to give her a childish bob as she took the small claw-like hand extended regally towards her, and she was abruptly glad that she was wearing a respectable skirt rather than jeans—and that her fingernails were clean.

Madame Merinard's first gesture of formality was to apologise for never having learned Sara's language. When Sara responded in flawless French she was rewarded with a further look of approval—and perhaps relief—which increased when Paul broke in from behind Sara to explain that Sara had grown up in France, and that her grandfather was Carl Farrow the conductor who had made his home in Paris. Not that her approval seemed to reach as far as Paul, because she was tapping an impatient finger on her chair-arm before he had finished speaking, in a way which almost seemed to reduce him to schoolboy status, and had turned back to Sara.

'I am sure Sara can speak for herself—I may address you as Sara?' She said it with the short a, in the French fashion. 'You have already met my grand-daughter Mylène Cougère, who is staying with us while her husband is away on business in Maroc.' The approval *definitely* didn't reach as far as Mylène, Sara noted, while she took in the information about Mylène with an echo of her former confusion. 'And my grandson has been employing you in that ridiculous house for some weeks without bringing you to see me, I gather.' A sharp look for Paul. 'He was no doubt thoughtless,' Madame Merinard added drily, 'because it doesn't seem to me a suitable place to have left you, and the housekeeper's death must certainly have been distressing for you. But never mind. We shall do our best to make you more comfortable here. I gather you have been put in the bedroom next to mine. Please don't worry if you hear me walking about during the night—at my age one needs little sleep, I find!'

'I hope that *I* shan't disturb you, madame,' Sara said respectfully, since some answer seemed to be expected of her.

'I'm sure you won't, as long as you don't play one of those transistor radios. I am not in the least hard of hearing—though I've often thought it would be an advantage,' Madame Merinard confided with a gleam of humour which had more than a touch of mischief in it, and drew an involuntary answering smile to Sara's face. 'Good,' the old lady said firmly, 'I can see we're going to understand each other. Paul, why are you frowning? I'm not aware that I've said anything to raise your disapproval, and you frown far too often!'

'Do I, Grandmère? I beg your pardon. And would I ever dare to disapprove of you?' he asked in a tone whose mock-meekness held affection—and which brought the glint of a smile into the old lady's eyes, however hard she tried to continue looking reproving.

'No doubt you were about to tell me that Sara has come here to work rather than to entertain *me*. Well, she shall work during the day, and tell me all about this history of Lorivel over dinner in the evenings—will that be a suitable compromise? It's possible to become bored,' Madame Merinard told Sara, continuing to ignore Mylène standing silently beside her, 'when one reaches my age and no-one makes conversation any more. Television—phu. It's a nonsense for the servant classes. The radio's little better. Paul can be entertaining, but he has been too wrapped up in his brain-child over recent months to pay much attention to anything else—or so it has seemed.' She ignored the sound of protest which came from behind Sara; though there was that touch of humour in her eyes again which suddenly suggested that this autocratic old lady enjoyed placing barbs here and there, as a game to amuse herself. 'Yes,' she said, studying Sara again with an odd thoughtfulness which reminded Sara sharply of the grandson at his most unfathomable, 'I am very glad that you have been brought to stay with me, Sara!'

Sara didn't dare to look round, though her awareness of Paul standing somewhere out of her eye-line was exasperating, disturbing, and only added to her sense of confusion. After last night, she might have expected almost anything rather than the bewilderment of being moved abruptly into a setting like this—formal as only the French knew how to be formal, with an old lady who looked as if she lived by rules out of another era. And with Mylène, who *wasn't* his wife. Not his wife but—the thought came unbidden and with a quiver of warning—someone who felt entitled to call him 'darling' and dance with her arms round his neck...Sara felt as if all her preconceived ideas of *anyone's* behaviour had been shaken up like a kaleidoscope without coming back to a readable pattern; but Madame Merinard was dismissing her graciously now, but telling Paul that she wanted to speak to him. As Sara left— and Mylène came with her—she couldn't even catch Paul's eye.

CHAPTER NINE

'Grandmère has taken one of her impulsive fancies to you,' Mylène said, leaning against the windowsill in the pose she always fell into, either by art or design. 'At her age, I suppose... and she does get so bored!'

'She's a very interesting person.' Sara made the answer short, wishing—as usual—that Mylène would go away. What *was* obvious was that Mylène was bored; at least whenever Paul was out of the house. Sara allowed the bitter-edged thought to intrude. Not his wife, no. Someone else's wife, yes. All the same, she believed in monopolising Paul's attention. At least she did whenever the grandmother wasn't there. There was a distinct tartness in the grandmother's attitude towards Mylène, and it was noticeable that the whole household—even Paul—didn't cross Madame Merinard.

He didn't out of affection, Sara thought, remembering the teasing gentleness and respect he showed towards the old lady. He had played cribbage with her for almost three hours last night, because she had insisted on going on until she won so thoroughly that there could be no argument about it.

'It's just as well I was able to drive you into Grasse to buy another couple of dresses for evening. Not that the shops there are much—but you wouldn't want to pay Cannes prices, would you?' Mylène gave her sweet, disdainful smile. 'Since she *will* insist on your eating with us, and she *will* insist on everyone changing for dinner, you had to have *something* to put on... Oh dear, Sara, am I disturbing you?'

'I've got to get this work done,' Sara said as politely as she could.

'You could do it in the evenings if only grandmère didn't insist on your always being there. I *had* thought,' Mylène said with a sigh, 'that with you here, Paul and I could have gone out. It's a pity she's in one of her moods to insist on seeing him too. Sometimes I think she has her own way too much! Oh dear, if only you *could* work in the evenings, you and I could drive down to the coast in this heat for a swim. But I suppose I'll have to go on my own. Paul wants you to get all those papers sorted out as soon as possible, I know. Ah well... Perhaps I'll just go and lie on the lawn for a bit, rather than driving. It's a pity you're missing all the sun, you're getting quite pale! I'll come and see how you're getting on a little later.'

She was always coming to see how Sara was getting on. She was always *there.* Sara couldn't imagine why she hung around the house when she could be elsewhere because, contrary to her first impression, Mylène didn't actually run the house: that was done by an efficient couple who had obviously been in Madame Merinard's service for years. Mylène, however, was a constant presence. She was there at breakfast. She was there when Paul left the house to go to the Lorivel works and always there when he returned; she was in the study with Sara at least half of every day; if she wasn't talking she was 'just curling up in the corner with a magazine'. It was a little like

252

being *haunted*, Sara thought with exasperation, and it had been like that for the whole of the last five days, so that—

It wasn't really any use saying to herself, so that Paul hadn't been able to talk to her, or she to him, because he hadn't tried to talk to her. Oh, he had been pleasant, impersonal, a little watchful, and socially perfectly attentive during the formal evening dinners which Madame Merinard presided over like a *grande dame*. She had thought... Sara swallowed hard, and admitted to herself that she had thought he might come to her bedroom. He hadn't. Well, he hardly would, with his grandmother next door making a habit of being wakeful at nights, but... She had to admit that he hadn't shown any signs of *wanting* to come anywhere near her. It was almost as if, as far as he was concerned, nothing had happened between them. She had tried telling herself that his withdrawn manner, his politeness, the mocking gleam she caught in his eye now and again, were all a deliberate way of punishing her for misjudging him enough to think he would have brought her to stay with his wife straight after spending the night with her. Certainly she had thought that on the first Sunday when he *could* have found time to talk to her alone and made a very obvious choice not to.

He treated Mylène with a polite and cousinly affection. But definitely affection.

If she made herself think back over all the weeks she had known him, Sara decided with a resolute attempt at firmness, she could see that he *was* extremely changeable.

It was probably, she knew bitterly, just her own inexperience which made her expect something more from him. If she sensed a tension in him, it was probably only because of work. It was no secret, here, that he was hoping to launch a new Lorivel classic soon. No secret either that it was his own work, *his* perfume, the product of *his* blending talents. She was glad for him, but took care not to ask questions, even when some remark of the grandmother's might have invited them. Mylène, she thought, didn't seem to take much interest—except for the occasional light comment that he was so *busy*—and the matter wasn't actually discussed, merely referred to in passing. Paul's attitude seemed a little like touching wood—don't talk about it in case it doesn't happen—and Sara could understand that. She felt an aching knowledge that she *did* understand him; or could; but that was probably just her own delusion.

It was no use pretending to herself that she didn't love him. If it had been an ache before, it was worse now; worse because she loved him more for seeing him in his own home setting, behaving with grace and patience to a very old lady, talking about everyday things, smiling, leaving for work in a hurry in the mornings...coming back in the evenings looking tired. Sara shook herself hard as if that would cure her, but knew that it wouldn't. It was like acting in a play not to give herself away but to answer all Madame Merinard's questions, and take part in conversations, in a coolly normal manner. She had to be a good actress, she thought grimly, not to show how she was swept with longing every time she glanced up to find Paul's eyes on her; and to answer his polite remarks with polite replies. It was just as well he couldn't know how often she lay awake at night with the ache a physical one, an intensity of feeling which was like a fever and gave her a wry knowledge of her own awakened nature. If it hadn't been for that, she might have begun to think she'd dreamed it...

She hadn't suggested again that she might leave. She told herself it was just because Madame Merinard was taking such a kind interest in her and she couldn't disappoint her. Madame was quite capable of producing memories about Lorivel's earlier days which drew the whole picture into focus, anyway— and Sara sometimes longed for a tape recorder when the old lady switched from asking questions about Sara's own family and life, to talking about something which had happened at Lorivel in Paul's grandfather's day. Perhaps she would produce some more of her fascinating sidelights tonight at dinner and give Sara something to fix her mind firmly on, instead of having to seek round for some distraction from the presence of Paul across the table. She *always* seemed to find herself seated opposite him—and she was getting tired of telling herself stubbornly that he wasn't as handsome as all that, certainly not handsome enough to take her appetite away through the formal series of quite deliciously-cooked courses. It was ironic that she'd always had a perfectly good appetite, through no matter what: now, when it showed, she hadn't.

Dinner began badly because Paul was late. Madame Merinard disapproved of lateness, for whatever reason, and Sara had to bite her tongue not to defend him as he answered his grandmother's querulous criticisms with patience in spite of having a drawn, tired look about him. Then Mylène said with pointed sulkiness that there was a film on she wanted to see which finished tonight and Paul *had* said he wanted to see it too—only to bring a snappish remark from the grandmother, with a complete change of attitude; that the man was tired and overworked, and couldn't Mylène see that instead of nagging? And he'd said he had had a puncture, didn't the girl hear him? It was almost involuntary when Sara caught Paul's eye with a rueful gleam in it and found herself giving him a tiny sympathetic smile.

Madame, however, seemed to have her temper much improved by squashing Mylène, and began, as Sara hoped she might, talking about her memories. Tonight, it was about coming to Lorivel as a bride. There had been a perfume named after her, too—'Chantal'—which had been a wedding present from her new husband: a good perfume, it had been, though out of fashion now. Gustav-Philippe had been two years younger than Paul was now when he married her, and he had only waited so long because *her* parents wouldn't agree to it at first, considering it a *mésalliance* because he was 'merely a *parfumier*'.' She gave Sara a wicked little smile with the words, obviously enjoying the memory of that stubborn courtship, and Sara grinned back at her.

'And you never regretted it, of course, madame!'

'Of course. I merely inspired Gustav-Philippe to become very successful, so that quite quickly he was much richer than my father and more important,' Madame said delightedly, and with a fine scorn. 'And the tradition of naming a perfume after the bride was carried on by my son—even if he waited a few years before he found one he thought good enough!'

'One can only take a classic when it comes, grandmère,' Paul told her; and added with mock-solemnity, 'But I'm comforted to know that if I take care to remain successful, I needn't think of myself as a misailliance! I've been worrying about it, naturally!'

'You know very well I think you should be married,' his grandmother told him waspishly. There was a tiny quaver, almost a plea if it had been from anyone less proud, as she added, 'The past is over—'

'Yes, indeed, grandmère. Over and done. So—'

'Talking of these classic perfumes of yours, have you had any more trouble with people trying to get into the works, Paul?' It was Mylène who broke in, with a high note in her voice which might have been excitement. 'It really *is* a repeat performance, isn't it, this spying business? I remember what happened to uncle Jacques—goodness, didn't your parents' marriage almost break up over it—when that girl was sent to spy on him, the very pretty one, who turned out in the end to be working with some man who wanted to get hold of a formula. For a German firm, was it? Or an American one? I forget which—but didn't she start out by picking him up on a train...?'

'I won't have such things discussed at my table, Mylène!' Madame Merinard said sharply—but Sara was gaping, her eyes going involuntarily to Paul's face, her mind whirling into sudden comprehension. She found she was closing her mouth very carefully as Paul gave her one look, then turned his head quickly to say something reassuring to his grandmother whose heightened colour showed that she was genuinely upset. Mylène said sulkily,

'Oh very well, I apologise, but it's all a long time ago now! It was when we were about fifteen, wasn't it, Paul—?'

'You were eighteen,' Paul said coldly over his shoulder, 'and you're old enough *now* not to discuss it in front of grandmère,' but his grandmother was speaking again with wavering dignity.

'I won't have dirty linen washed in public,

and if you have no better manners than to do so, Mylène, then you can leave the room!'

'In public? Oh, in front of someone who's supposed to be writing the Lorivel history—I see—sorry!'

It was perhaps the touch of spite in Mylène's voice which made Sara find her own; or perhaps it was a quick pity for the old lady's distress. In the era which Madame Merinard chose to recreate, and particularly in the fierce Catholicism she sometimes displayed, such family crises were *not* discussed publicly. Sara leaned forward, and found herself saying gently, and with only the barest trace of irony in her voice,

'I can assure you, madame, that I would never write about anything so—'

'So vulgar. No, I'm sure you would not.' Madame Merinard had herself in hand now, though her colour was high and her eyes bright. 'Thank you, Sara, I would expect no less—from *you*.' She didn't look at her granddaughter, still seated at the end of the table, but lifted her fork with a hand which had only the barest shake. 'We will continue with our meal, and talk about something else. Sara, my dear, you seem to have very little appetite, is there something lighter you would prefer to have cooked for you? I've noticed that you pick at your food, and I'm sure you should take more nourishment!'

'I'm very healthy, thank you, madame. It's just that when one sits down all day, one doesn't get hungry. But the food is excellent, of course!' She certainly wasn't hungry *now*, and it seemed just the wrong moment for madame to point it out.

'We should see that you take more exercise. I'm sure there's no need for you to work as hard as you do! Paul—'

'Tonight I do have a headache, madame,' Sara said very quickly, 'I wonder if you'd mind if I asked you to excuse me and went up to my room?' She had managed not to look at Paul again: she went on managing it as she got to her feet with madame's sympathetic permission. It was quite an effort to leave the room slowly and with the decorum she knew madame would expect, but at last she *was* out of it. She made for the stairs—and was three steps up then when she heard the dining-room door open again and close sharply.

'Sara!'

She turned and looked down at him, with no need now to put a guard on the anger of her expression. The look he gave her held resignation, and an acknowledgement that her guess was inevitably correct, as he came to stand looking up at her, but there was—of all things—a dancing amusement in his dark eyes.

'It only goes to show that *I* can jump to the wrong conclusions just as quickly as you can—'

'Don't stop me,' she said icily, but keeping her voice low in case the grandmother's acute hearing should catch the sounds of a quarrel, 'I'm just going up to report on my two-way radio! You wouldn't like to give me any vital information to pass on, I suppose—?'

'Stop being angry and laugh about it instead,' he invited, coaxingly, 'after all I'm the one who ended up looking a fool, aren't I? And *don't* start threatening to leave again, because you're not going—grandmère would never forgive me, you know—'

'Leave me alone!' she said quickly, because

he had taken a step up the stairs towards her.

'I'm at the end of my patience on leaving you alone. And why on earth you have to be stowed at *that* end of the house—'

'*You* probably still think I'm a spy!' she hissed fiercely.

'No I don't. But you must admit, it did look a bit suspicious the way you disappeared unexpectedly for two days between leaving London and coming here! And then Matthew Gaunt turned out not to know an awful lot about you—except that you'd worked for him for eight months and that—well, that he liked you—'

'So *you* immediately decided I'd disappeared to be briefed, and that I had a murky past! Just when was I supposed to have planned all this,' she asked with heavy sarcasm, 'considering it all came up by chance? Or did you think I made a habit of it? Yes, I suppose you did!'

'Do we have to discuss it now? And right here? After all,' he said, looking as if his patience was wearing thin but still with that infuriating gleam of amusement in his eyes, 'I have very good reason to know that you weren't sent here to seduce me, don't I? It's hardly likely that—'

The opening of the dining-room door cut him off just in time, and Mylène's voice came to them with clear, cross urgency. She said, 'Paul, you'd better come, grandmère's not feeling very well and needs helping up to bed. Oh, are you still there, Sara? I thought you had *such* a headache?'

Paul turned away, going swiftly back to see his grandmother, the door closing behind both him and Mylène. Sara—feeling thankful that Mylène too was a non-English-speaker—was torn between wanting to go back and see if she could help, and wanting to take refuge in her room fast. She chose the latter, because there would be very little she could do for madame, and she didn't want to risk any more discussion with Paul. In fact—grandmother next door or no—she locked her door. And, for the first time, found herself feeling thankful that Mylène was always around. If there was one thing she didn't want, she told herself fiercely, it was to hear Paul casually explaining just why he'd decided she wasn't an

265

experienced seductress.

She knew she would forgive him in the end, however hard she tried to hold on to her feeling of anger. In fact he was right, and it was funny, that they could have started out at such cross-purposes. Every innocent question Sara had asked out of curiosity must have made matters worse. She could see that now. All the same, she wasn't going to let him pass it off so lightly, she decided with a firm resolve which countered her sudden desire to giggle. Perhaps it was true that they were quits—but he could apologise. After that...

She didn't examine what would happen after that, but she felt remarkably light-hearted when she went downstairs in the morning, though she didn't go down until she was sure Paul would have left. She allowed herself a touch of worry about Madame Merinard's health, though she had heard the old lady saying audibly but querulously as she passed her door last night that she *didn't* need the doctor, all she wanted was to have an early night for once. When Sara went down, no-one was around except the servants, appearing with prompt efficiency and with no complaint about her lateness to offer her *café-au-lait* and brioches or toast if she would prefer it.

It was mid-morning for once before Mylène came wandering into the study. She was looking very bad-tempered. Sara—who had been finding it very hard to concentrate—tried to look pleasant but busy, as she looked up to ask politely,

'How is Madame Merinard this morning?'

'Oh, she's perfectly all right! She'll probably outlive all of us! Feeling ill's a form of blackmail with her,' Mylène said, with such a sharp note in her voice that Sara was almost shocked. 'All I was trying to do was deflect her away from that endless subject of Paul getting married, which she does go on about so! I'd forgotten that she lives in such a different century from the rest of us that one mustn't mention anything shocking in front of her. Particularly not anything about darling Uncle Jacques, of course, her only son amongst all those daughters!'

Sara couldn't think of any answer to make, so she kept silent. Mylène, she thought, wasn't just looking cross, she was looking unhappy: no doubt she had been hearing the rough side of her grandmother's tongue as usual. While Sara hadn't managed to find Mylène likeable, she couldn't help feeling a certain sympathy for her; and if she had often had the feeling that Mylène used her as an audience rather than taking any real interest in her, she tried to feel sympathy for the discontent which led to that, too. After a moment she asked, simply as a friendly gesture,

'Will your husband be coming back from his business trip soon?'

'He's not away at all, he's at home in Orleans! The other's just a fiction of grand-mère's.' The words came out on a high note of exasperation, and she gave Sara an almost pleading look out of those fine, expressive eyes which she always used to such great effect. 'You can see what the situation really is, can't you? It's just that grandmère won't admit it. She knows I have left Charles—she knows I never should have married him in the first place—but she's so old-fashioned—'

'She's old,' Sara pointed out, since Mylène

268

had broken off and seemed to expect some answer.

'She's not too old to know that some Catholics have their marriages annulled. But oh dear me no, she doesn't want to admit it might happen in her family.' Mylène took a distracted turn round the room. 'And of course, she doesn't want it for Paul either!'

'For—Paul?' Sara said very carefully, in a voice whose steadiness had nothing to do with the way her stomach had suddenly turned over.

'Well, of course. We've always been in love with each other, ever since we were young. It doesn't end,' Mylène said tragically, 'not for either of us, however hard we've tried, because the family was against it. Perhaps, because you're English, you can't understand how—how archaic it can still be here! I was pushed into marrying Charles, and—well, obviously it could never work! But I did try. I swear to you, Sara, I tried to be a good wife. But you've seen how it is for Paul and me, how right we are together! Oh, he's very careful to hide how he feels in front of grandmère, of course, because he does feel it's his duty not to hurt her. I've *told* him that in the end the only thing is to come out into the open, and make her face it—but he has such a thing about the family, you know! And all the time he and I...well, why do you think he's never married, when he's had every girl in the neighbourhood after him ever since he grew up?'

'I thought he was engaged once,' Sara said, the words coming out coldly.

'Oh, that. Such a silly little chit, that Ysabel. Did you know that she drowned herself when she had to recognise that he didn't really love her? You'd have thought she'd have recognised it,' Mylène said callously, 'after all he's never pretended to be a saint.'

Sara felt very sick suddenly. It was so close to being a physical thing that she had to put her hand over her mouth. She wished she could put her hands over her ears as Mylène went on speaking. 'Of course he's always had a lot of women,' she said with cool practicality, if with a touch of bitterness, 'what man doesn't, when it's there on offer? And with his charm he's always been able to get anyone he wanted. And since they wouldn't let him have me... But now grandmère's really started this marriage thing again. How it's time he settled down. How she wants to see her great-grand-children before she dies.' There was a very bitter twist in Mylène's mouth. 'It's because I'm here, of course, and she's beginning to be afraid he won't toe the line after all, that this time... But what I'm afraid of is that he will toe the line, and be miserable!'

'I shouldn't think he ever does anything he doesn't want to do,' Sara said drily. It was odd to find her voice sounding quite normal, when the rest of her seemed to have gone away somewhere, into some limbo from which she could look down with detachment. 'Mylène, if you wouldn't mind, I really have got work to do. And none of this,' she said steadily, 'is—is really any of my business!'

'No, but it's such a comfort to be able to talk to someone. I knew you'd understand, because we're the same generation, aren't we? And I know you're not really so sweet and demure as you pretend to be with grandmère,' Mylène said, with enough spite in it to spoil

271

the sweet note she was trying to put in her voice.

'All the same—'

'Yes, all right, I'll go away and let you work! It's just so stifling here, with grandmère keeping on asking me when I'm going back to Charles—yes, all right, dear Sara, I am going!'

She drifted away, on a waft of rather strong perfume which was presumably something from Lorivel, and the door closed gently behind her. Sara stared at the letter in her hand—which must have been in her hand all the time—and, almost automatically, filed it and picked up another one. Then very suddenly she remembered that Madame Merinard had told her she ought to take more exercise, so decided she would go out for a walk. She would go into the village, and perhaps further if she could find a path which led into the wilder country. It didn't matter where, as long as she could move.

She walked for quite a long way. The wild country was extremely scenic, but she didn't really notice it. She walked, sat amongst the heather for a while, walked again. Her head seemed to be remarkably empty. The only idea she could really catch hold of, as she made her way back, was to decide with a peculiar lightness that she had grown up. She had just turned into the entrance of the manor's formal drive when a car drew up beside her with a crunch of gravel. It was only early afternoon, but somehow there was no particular surprise in seeing Paul. He smiled at her, leaned over to push open the passenger door, and said amiably, 'Hop in.'

'I'm out for a walk,' Sara said politely, 'so I'll walk, thank you.'

One corner of his mouth went down, one eyebrow went up, and he gave her a mock-patient look. When she didn't respond, his eyes narrowed, though he said quite mildly, 'I came home to talk to you.'

'Really? For any particular reason?'

'Don't sulk, Sara!'

'Goodness me, no. By the way, I decided you were right, and it was funny—thinking I was a spy, I mean!'

'Ah! It's not that, then. Sure you think it's funny?'

'One of many amusing things.' She found that she was looking at him as if examining him under a microscope: incredibly handsome, yes; charming and spoiled; not really at all the sort of person to be as star-crossed as Mylène described, but no doubt he was very good at hiding his *real* feelings. She found that he was looking back at her with a baffled, slightly irritated expression, and he said with a sudden edge of challenge in his deep voice, 'You will talk to me, either here or somewhere else, and if it's going to be a screaming match perhaps it'd better be somewhere else! So get in the car, unless you want me to drag you in!'

'I don't actually go much for violence—'

'Still holding that against me? Darling, please try to remember that I only started out in an awful temper—'

She didn't like the 'darling', nor the weak feeling it gave her, so that she was stung into a rapid retort. 'Oh, I've forgotten all about that,' she said very lightly, 'why are you making so much of it? After all it wasn't really important, was it? A writer ought to have experienced everything, and I thought it was about time I did, that's all! Thanks—'

'*Thanks?*' he said murderously. She had seen the shock her words caused him, and the opaque blackness of his eyes was enough to make her want to flinch. She felt as if everything had gone into slow motion as she watched him clamp down on his temper and she waited to hear his sardonic, cutting retort. It never came: instead he slammed the car door and the vehicle flew into motion so fast that a spray of gravel hit her like bullets. He swung the car round, cutting a sharp mark into the carefully tended lawn as he went, and was out through the gate while she was still wondering if he was going to hit the near post. Definitely a man in a temper.

A man who wasn't used to being taken lightly.

It seemed like a small triumph. It also seemed like an incredibly empty one.

He might be in love with Mylène, but he was used to the rest of the world fawning round him. Particularly women. Even killing themselves for love of him, Sara thought with sick bitterness. Poor Ysabel, to have expected so much of him!

She found she was walking back up to the house. That she was sitting down and going on with her work. She didn't really know why. It just seemed like something to do.

Paul was out for dinner. He was also out for the whole of Sunday—and so, noticeably, was Mylène—and then they were both out again on Monday night. And on Tuesday. He must, Sara thought bitterly, have suddenly decided to stop keeping the whole thing such a secret; though she found herself going along with the grandmother's desire to pretend that the cousins weren't actually out together as the old lady lapsed into fretfulness at everyone's sudden absence and leaned on Sara's company with sudden pathos. With such determination, too, that it would have been both ill-mannered and impossible to do anything other than try to fill Madame Merinard's evenings with talking and listening and playing the two-handed patience she insisted on teaching Sara. Paul must be leaving very early in the mornings and coming back very late because Sara somehow managed not to see him at all; and while

Mylène was occasionally visible she had suddenly stopped hanging round Sara, exchanging it for a burst of frenetic activity which took her out of the house during the day as well as in the evenings. Sara found she was being summoned to keep the grandmother company from teatime onwards, and it was the old lady's temporary dependence on her, she knew, which was making her so indecisive about leaving. It was very much easier to let herself drift than to make the decision from which she flinched, anyway—even if she was wryly aware that it was a self-inflicted indulgence to let herself be shown photograph albums containing far too many photographs of Paul as a child, Paul as a young boy, Paul as a teenager.

Unfortunately, what the old lady liked to do most in his absence was talk about Paul. That there was a pointed quality in her comments—and in her attempts to draw comments in response from Sara—only got through to Sara as she was changing for yet another dinner-for-two on Thursday evening. She had just slipped the short apricot chiffon dress over her head with an automatic gesture, and was thinking wryly but absently that all this dressing-for-dinner-with-madame was as unreal as stepping back into history and had nothing to do with her own life at all, when a sudden cold suspicion caught at her and pierced through the limbo in which she seemed to have been existing. No, it wasn't possible! Madame might be a stubborn old lady who made the arbitrary choice to favour Sara with her approval—she might be inclined to make endless enquiries about Sara's family background and choose to approve of that too—but she couldn't have decided that...

She was always going on about the fact that it was time Paul married: Mylène had said so!

Anyway she wouldn't choose...

Sara gave a little shiver. If madame had decided in her autocratic fashion that here was a suitable wife for her grandson, she thought bitterly, she couldn't have made a worse decision. And, as Mylène would say, it was archaic to think about grandmothers trying to arrange marriages in this day and age. But then madame was archaic, quite deliberately so. All at once Sara felt extraordinarily stifled. She should never have got mixed up with these Merinards at all, she thought painfully. And perhaps she should try to say something tonight, drop some hint about Paul and Mylène...except that it would only upset the grandmother and she would probably refuse to believe it. It must be comforting, she thought with sudden bitterness, to be able to shut your eyes to anything you didn't want to see. She would certainly have to make her decision about leaving if madame really had taken hold of such an idea; and she knew that it would be difficult to face Madame across the table and talk normally now that the suspicion had come to her. But at least Paul wouldn't be there, because she had seen as she passed that the dining-table was laid for only two again.

She found she was a fraction late, was forgiven, and sat down in her place. Madame made some sharp, irritable grumble about Myléne using the place as a hotel but ignored the fact that Paul too was missing. Then the door opened, heralding the arrival of more cutlery and glass instead of soup. And then Paul.

Sara didn't know why she had been telling herself that she'd forgotten what he looked like: once he was there, all dark intensity and smooth elegance, she knew she could have recited every line of his features. He hadn't even sat down before Madame Merinard, concealing pleasure behind temper but developing a sparkle in her manner which hadn't been there before, was greeting him with.

'Ah, you've decided to honour us with your company again, have you!'

'Have I been missed?' He didn't look at Sara, but kept his eyes on his grandmother, adding merely, 'Mylène not in?'

'She's been out all week, just like you have!'

'Really? Oh yes, I remember she said something about meeting up with some old friends,' Paul said casually. 'Some of the people she knew in the old days, I think.'

'She should go home to her husband. I don't know why he lets her racket around the way she does!'

'Oh, allow her some fun, grandmère. I shouldn't imagine Charles is very easy to live with—you've always said he was dull,

280

haven't you?'

'All the same. She's been away from him too long.' There was a distinct challenge in the words—and Sara waited on a sudden indrawn breath for some response from Paul, but he merely shrugged.

'Allow other people their marriages. I expect she'll go home soon. Has the work been going well, Sara?'

She almost jumped at the polite question, which was offered in an impersonal tone. 'Yes—thank you,' she said after a fractional pause.

'Sara has been keeping *me* company a great deal, which shows what a good girl she is. And makes up a great deal for my own family's neglect!' Madame Merinard said with the same challenge; to which this time Paul responded with a smile. If it had an edge of mockery on it, unusual in the way he addressed his grandmother, perhaps that was something to do with the very plain look of approval Madame Merinard had given Sara, she thought with embarrassment; but he was speaking.

'I do have to work, you know, grandmère!

You'd be the first to tell me off if I didn't pay attention to Lorivel, wouldn't you? How am I to keep it as successful as you and grandfather made it, if I don't keep an eye on things? As for the rest of my time,' he went on in a voice which sounded casual, but was somehow deliberate, 'you keep telling me that I ought to settle down, so I thought I'd do another survey of the local talent.'

'That's a highly unsuitable way of putting it,' Madame Merinard snapped; but he merely smiled at her again.

'Is it? Well, you'll just have to forgive me, since I've only been trying to please you! Let's see, on Sunday I went out with Béatrice Louvel. Then on Monday, Linda—no, I don't believe you'd know Linda's family, but she's half American. On Tuesday it was Christine Seyrac, whose father sends you his regards, by the way. And then on Wednesday—'

'You can spare us a further list of your conquests,' his grandmother snapped, looking really annoyed now, but adding with a snort, 'At least you can't have found one to please you if you went on taking out a different one every night!'

'You know how difficult I am to please,' he said smoothly, 'and I have to admit, I didn't immediately decide I wanted to marry Béatrice, or Linda, or Christine. Which is a pity when you pointed out to me only the other day that I'm getting too old to wait much longer. Never mind, perhaps the next batch—'

'You're better ignored when you're in this mood,' his grandmother told him, glancing suspiciously at the blandness of his expression and the spots of colour on each cheek. 'And I'm not at all surprised to see Sara looking annoyed—'

'Oh, I'm not at all annoyed, madame! Just interested! I always thought it was only teenagers who felt they had to boast.'

The words brought a crow of laughter from Madame Merinard. Sara, who had meant to disconcert Paul or at least irritate him for playing what sounded like a childish game of, 'You see, some women want me,' was irritated herself when he gave her a look just as innocent as hers had been at him.

'Ah, but you don't understand, Sara, it's not

a question of boasting, but of demonstrating to my grandmother that I really am trying! She's been threatening to find me a wife for at least a couple of years now, if I won't find one for myself.'

'And could do it a great deal better than you, no doubt!'

'You haven't finished your list by telling us who it was on Wednesday!' Sara said rapidly—and brightly, to cover her embarrassment because Paul's eyes were still on her, and, because Madame Merinard had cast a glance in her direction which seemed to hold too much meaning.

'Oh, on Wednesday I worked. All evening. We've started production,' Paul said, turning towards his grandmother after what seemed an extraordinarily thoughtful study of Sara's face, and giving a sudden, open smile. 'I decided the test run was successful enough to go ahead. And now that we've got this far, shall I describe my new perfume to you? Not that words can really give you the flavour, but...for Sara's benefit, just so that she's quite sure I don't think she's an enemy agent,

I'll try—'

'Enemy agent? What nonsense is that?'

'Just a joke between us, grandmère. Now then. It's lighter than most of our lines when you first smell it, younger perhaps, fresh and sweet without being cloying. Then underneath, coming out later, there's a deeper tone—with something a little mysterious about it? No, it's no use, I can't describe it, you'll have to wait until I can demonstrate it. But it's worked as I hoped it would, on the two levels, and they gradually blend without losing either quality.'

'Hmph,' was all the grandmother said—though Sara felt she could have made a greater response to the enthusiasm which was there in Paul's face, the look of tentative pride and excitement which made her forget everything else she knew about him in the sudden longing to put her arms round him in congratulation. 'And what are you going to call it?' Madame Merinard demanded.

'Ah, that...can stay a secret for the moment. Or perhaps I haven't quite decided. There are some parts of my life which you must allow me to run for myself, grandmère,' he told her with a sudden brilliant smile which brought out all his charm, and which silenced the protest the old lady was obviously just about to make. And then he changed the subject with an abrupt firmness which wouldn't be denied, and went on making conversation about other things through the rest of the meal. He even drew Sara in by talking about music, and the time he had actually been to one of Carl Farrow's concerts when he was an undergraduate in Lyons.

She was far from proof against his charm, when he chose to turn it on. It felt quite unreal to be sitting talking to him with all the undercurrents of knowledge and feeling which swirled round inside her and which made her feel as if she was living two separate lives both at once. She kept being caught by the delusion that this was just a normal, friendly evening spent with the man she loved and his grandmother. In the end, after Madame had tried rather too pointedly to throw the two of them together and had been challenged to a hand of picquet by her grandson instead, Sara managed to drift out onto the terrace through the open glass doors. It was a hot night and if an excuse were needed, she'd have said she needed more air. It was easier out here in the dark to let her guard down and give in to a feeling of aching wistfulness, and bewilderment, and anger. She made herself wonder why he was home for the evening without Mylène; how he could manage to sound so casual about Mylène; whether he had really been out with all those other girls this week or whether it was just a cover up. He probably had, she decided angrily as she drifted down from the terrace onto the lawn and began to walk about amongst the formal rose-garden. And he probably would make a nice, safe, dynastic marriage with one of them to please his grandmother. He certainly wasn't going to marry her to please his grandmother... The thought brought some highly unladylike and modern swearwords to her lips which gave her the satisfaction of feeling that no, she wasn't as sweet and demure as grandmère thought her, and she wasn't about to be mixed up in any old-fashioned rural French nonsense about arranged marriages either—but it also brought the muddled ache back into her heart and she tried to bury it in a quick turn round the dark bulk of the small summer-house which stood in the middle of the formal rose-garden.

She would go, she thought suddenly. She would just up and leave. Not this minute, because she could hardly take off in the middle of the night into the middle of the countryside wearing a chiffon cocktail dress and with no transport and no luggage. She would lock herself into her room tonight and go tomorrow. She must go, because she had the sudden shivering conviction that if Paul Merinard did decide to marry to please his grandmother—if he decided in his casual lordly way to marry her to please his grandmother—then she'd just weakly say yes. In spite of Mylène. In spite of poor callously treated Ysabel. She was that much of an idiot!

She heard her name being called from the terrace, and shrank back against the summer-house hoping she was invisible here in the dark. She must be, because after a moment Paul went back inside again. Sara waited for several minutes, and then walked swiftly round the house to let herself in by the side door so that she could reach her room without meeting anyone.

CHAPTER TEN

London seemed grey and featureless despite too many buildings and too much city grime. Sara told herself that it was only the contrast, and the fact that London was having a wet June to make it seem all the more depressing after the glowing warmth of the South of France.

Even the flat didn't seem the welcome and familiar refuge she'd imagined it would be. Bet, of course, greeted Sara with surprise and pleasure—but very soon stopped her flood of excited, animated questions and became, instead, quietly and practically sympathetic with a careful lack of curiosity. She accepted Sara's explanation for her sudden return—that Mr Halberson had died before she even arrived and then the housekeeper's illness and death had left her nowhere to work—without comment. She merely looked thoughtful when Sara added that she wasn't able to get enough co-operation from—anyone—to do the writing she'd meant to do, and she didn't want to waste her time on what turned into merely a filing job. When Sara didn't immediately ring Gaunt Press to get her old job back, but went out and signed up with an agency for temporary typing work which produced an immediate job which *was* mainly filing, Bet didn't comment on that, either.

Leaving the manor and travelling back to England had been so unexpectedly simple that it was almost, Sara thought, as if fate approved of her decision and smoothed her path. She hadn't even decided which way to go, but the lorry in which she hitched a lift had turned out to be going to Nice, and had dropped her at the airport. There had been a cancellation on a flight to London and she had been allowed to pay for her ticket with her credit card. It had all been remarkably easy. She had been back in England almost before she'd had time to think about it.

She didn't *want* to think about it. She

wanted to live from day to day and wait for her bruised heart to recover. It would, eventually, she told herself stubbornly: no-one ever died of love. The phrase reminded her abruptly of Ysabel—and she knew that she had been wrong about Ysabel, that Mylène had given her a twisted version of the truth. The real truth—about that—had been unexpectedly revealed to her just before she left the manor; and Sara couldn't help knowing that it explained some of Paul's sardonic manner and his cynicism. She found herself looking back over that unexpected conversation with his grandmother.

Madame Merinard never emerged from her room in the mornings, so that Sara had expected to be able to go without seeing her, aiming to leave a polite and apologetic message with the servants. She had waited to hear Paul go off to work, listening for his car. Shortly after that, and showing that madame *was* awake, she had heard an altercation break out abruptly next door which ended when Mylène, whose muffled voice had been clearly recognisable, had slammed out of the house.

The sound somehow made Sara move all the more hastily to stuff the last pieces of her packing into the corners of her case. When a tap came at her door, she had jumped guiltily—and had been even more disconcerted when the servant who entered brought a polite request for her to go to see Madame Merinard in her room. It was, of course, more of a summons than a request and couldn't be refused. Sara looked down dubiously at her jeans and shirt—and then decided with a touch of stubbornness that Madame would have to see her as she was, a modern girl from this part of this century. She went to knock at the door of the next-door bedroom making a quick preparation of what she would say, now that she had to face Madame in person; and refused to let herself feel daunted by the sight of the old lady sitting up in bed against a lacy pillow, with an elegant bed-jacket draped round her shoulders and her white hair already brushed up into its faultless coronet.

'I'm glad that I have had the chance to see you, madame. I'm afraid I have to go back to England today, because I've had a message about an important job waiting for me. The work I'm doing sorting out the papers here is—is really almost done, and I mustn't miss the chance of something which could forward my writing career. My career *is* very important to me,' Sara added firmly, wondering a little why madame was regarding her without any annoyance. 'I want to thank you for—'

'Yes, yes,' madame interrupted, 'If you want to go to England, Sara, I'm sure Paul can arrange it for you. Or perhaps it can be dealt with over the telephone? You must ask him. He said last night that he will come back at about half-past three today to take you up to Lorivel. So that you can see round the works, and smell his new perfume.' Her eyes sparkled for a second, but then her expression became grave. 'However, I want to talk to you first, that's why I have sent for you. Sit down, please.'

She patted a chair beside her bed. Sara came forward unwillingly, her heart giving an uneasy beat which she tried to quell. 'But, madame,' she began stubbornly, 'I'm afraid I *have* to—'

'Sit. All the rest—' A little wave of the hand dealt with whatever Sara wanted to say—'can be dealt with later. I want to talk to you about something Paul won't say to you—and don't interrupt!' she added with her old imperious sharpness as Sara opened her mouth. 'It isn't my habit to discuss family matters, but I think you should be told about the girl Ysabel Renard who was once engaged to Paul.' As Sara shut her mouth, madame gave her a sharp glance. 'You've heard the name?'

'I—yes, madame, but—'

'Then you've probably heard scandal rather than truth. People always prefer it. And Paul refused to counter any rumours—for the Renards' sake, though I've always felt personally that he owes them nothing! If they hadn't over-indulged the child she wouldn't have run wild.' There was scorn in madame's voice, but concern in her eyes too—for Paul, Sara guessed. 'Ysabel and Paul became engaged with the blessing of both families. She was—oh, nineteen or twenty I suppose, and a pretty enough little thing. It wasn't mentioned to *us* that she had been brought home to keep her out of bad company, and certainly she seemed— Never mind, there's no point in making it into a long story. Once she was engaged to Paul her parents allowed her more freedom again. Unfortunately,' the grandmother said with unconcealed pain in her eyes, 'at that time my son died very suddenly. Paul took over at Lorivel, and had to be very busy because they were in the middle of some...oh, some negotations of some sort. He couldn't spend the time with Ysabel, and she slipped back into her old habits with some of her old friends. There was a swimming party at somebody's house, to which Paul was not invited. They were all drinking too much and taking—stimulants of some kind. As a result Ysabel drowned. At the inquest it was said—'

'You really don't have to tell me any more, madame!' Sara said quickly.

'No? You're aware of the effects of these stimulants mixed with alcohol? Yes, I suppose nowadays everyone does know about these things,' madame paused for a second, disapproval mixed with sadness in her eyes. It was as if she was looking back at her own, more innocent world with regret—though she surprised Sara a moment later by adding, 'There were foolish people in my day too, but perhaps the dangers weren't so readily available. And of course, in Ysabel's case there was more—and this is something the family has always been careful not to tell me, since it was hushed up. But do they really think I don't have my own sources of information?' There was disdain in her voice. 'When it concerns my own family, I certainly believe in knowing all the truth. Ysabel was pregnant when she died—and not by Paul. There were several young men in her life, as it turned out. That, of course, hit him hard—he's as proud as anyone else.'

'Thank you for telling me, madame,' Sara said in a small voice, after a silence had stretched so long that she felt she had to say something. Madame seemed to come back to the present with a start, and gave Sara a sharp, thoughtful look out of her slanting dark eyes.

'I thought you should know. I shall tell him that I've told you. He may be angry with me for being an interfering old woman, but that's better than allowing you to be worried by the fact that he's sometimes moody, hm? There've been scandalmongers to say the girl didn't die by accident, but there's no doubt that she did. When my family are so careful not to tell me things, I make sure my sources are impeccable.' The old lady said the words quite gravely, as if it was natural that she should have her own sources of accurate information since this was only her rightful due. Sara found that she had no doubt at all that madame did know everything—everything she chose to know. 'She would have been a most unsuitable wife for Paul,' Madame said firmly—and with a shade too much meaning, so that Sara was relieved when the grandmother leaned back against her pillows and added, 'I'm a little tired now. The morning's a far better time for sleeping than the night, I find. You may leave me now, Sara. But don't forget that Paul will come this afternoon to take you to Lorivel!'

Looking back at that conversation now, Sara couldn't help hoping that Madame Merinard hadn't been too angry to find she'd gone after all. Madame was used to getting her own way, and there had been something in her manner which suggested she'd reached the point of feeling satisfied she was going to get it this time. It didn't seem to occur to her, Sara thought bitterly—or perhaps she just didn't think it important—that it would be very difficult for someone to be married to Paul when he was really in love with his cousin Mylène...particularly if that someone loved him to distraction herself. It was one thing to have the truth about Ysabel sorted out—but there was still Mylène.

Her misery would pass, Sara told herself stubbornly. She would stop missing Paul. She would stop wondering what he was doing and thinking, and she would stop having this craven feeling that it would be better to be with him under any circumstances than not to see him at all. Goodness me, three months ago she hadn't even met the man. She had her career to fight for, and her ambitions to absorb her, because she would still go on trying to be a writer of course whether she ever got married or not. If she couldn't feel like even wanting to write anything just now, that would soon

come back. She just had to go through the
motions of living at the moment, going out
of the flat in the mornings to her boring and
mundane temporary job, coming back again
in the evenings...

Trying not to count the days since she left
France. That wasn't so easy, Sara thought
dispiritedly as she climbed the stairs to the flat
saying 'Ten' to herself to mark off yet another
slow day. She was late tonight, because the
lizard-like man from Sales had insisted on
having an extra letter typed at the last
moment—and had then lurked round Sara's
desk showing a tendency to lean over her unnecessarily, until she gave him such a frosty
look that he practically flinched and walked
away looking huffy. Perhaps he'd get her sacked, Sara thought hopefully, on the excuse that
her work wasn't good enough so the agency
had better send someone else. And perhaps if
that happened she'd find the energy to stop
marking time and do something a bit more
constructive. She put her key in the door and
let herself into the flat, catching sight of herself
in the hall mirror and deciding that her tan was

beginning to fade to an unbecoming yellow. Or perhaps it was getting washed off by the persistent drizzle: either way, it went well with the dark lines under her eyes. She had just pulled her raincoat off and put her umbrella down when Bet suddenly came out of the living-room, pulling the door shut behind her and saying,

'Oh, you're home, thank goodness! I was beginning to wonder where you'd got to! There's someone in there to see you—and *I'm* going out!' she added in a rush.

She gave Sara a push towards the living-room door, before Sara could do more than wonder why her normally placid friend should be giving her an oddly shiny and approving look. Perhaps Mr Gaunt had heard she was back and had actually come round to the flat to see her: that would please Bet who, Sara knew, must be thinking she ought to pull herself together. She opened the door and took two steps into the room—and stopped, with the abrupt feeling that the floor had given way under her.

Paul was standing quite still in the middle

of the room, looking darkly handsome and exotically out of place in its ordinary shabbiness, and watching her with those unfathomable dark eyes.

Sara supposed she must have shut the door, since she found she was leaning against it. He watched her for a moment longer as if waiting for her to say something, and for one hysterical moment Sara thought he was going to say, 'We still have a contract, Miss Farrow!' Instead, in that slightly sardonic but velvety voice she had never expected to hear again, he said,

'Why is it, d'you suppose, that every time I tell myself I'm never going to speak to you again, I find myself coming looking for you?'

'*Paul*—?'

'I'm certainly not a ghost. Your friend was able to see me. We've just spent half an hour talking to each other. No, let's start with the essentials, for once!' Suddenly he was moving, and before Sara knew what was happening she had been pulled away from the door and into his arms. When his lips found hers unerringly she knew it was because she had lifted her face involuntarily to his, and his kiss was strong and hard and thorough and brought back all the melting longing she had been trying so hard to forget. He pulled her down onto the settee and kissed her again, then cupped her chin with his hand to make her look at him.

'*Now* look me in the eye and tell me you don't love me!'

'I—can't—'

'Then what on earth did you run away for? What was the matter *this* time?' His lips brushed hers lightly, and then he put her a little away from him, though he kept a firm possessive hold on her as he studied her out of eyes which had a light in them, but puzzlement too. 'You're such a little hellcat, Sara, under that sweet manner of yours—am I ever going to understand you? Tell me!'

'I just wanted to come home—'

'Nonsense!'

'All right, then—'

'Grandmère told you about Ysabel,' he said abruptly, adding with some of his old cynicism, 'in detail, I gather. Did that put you off? I can't quite see why. It's a long time in the past. And it isn't anything I did, except—that it probably wouldn't have happened if I'd given her more of my time. There were reasons—'

Sara found that she was putting a finger against his lips: she couldn't bear to hear him blaming himself, in the circumstances. 'No, of course it wasn't that,' she said huskily.

'But something. My evil temper? I really was very jealous that night. And I'd been so worried—' He must have caught something in her expression which told him it wasn't that, because he broke off, watching her alertly, almost humorously. 'It is something to do with that wretched grandmother of mine, I'd swear it. I'd do a great deal to please her, but sometimes I could also strangle her— Ah. Now I said something there which made you flinch. I've never actually strangled anyone, darling, in case you think I have!'

'I know about you and Mylène,' Sara said sharply. If there was a part of her which was pleading to take whatever he offered, there was another, more stubborn part which refused to give in to illusion—no matter what it cost. 'I know that you're in love with each other. She told me. All about how the family didn't approve so she married someone else—and how she wants to get a divorce and marry you but you wouldn't hurt your grandmother that much—and your grandmother wants you to get married,' she went on in a rush, 'and you needn't think I don't know who she'd decided to pick out to be the s-sacrificial lamb, because she was making that far too clear!'

He was wearing an odd expression: there was anger in it, and exasperation, but also something else she couldn't read. His hands were still holding her—not tightly, but she had more than a suspicion that if she tried to move away he wouldn't let her. He didn't even bother to deny what she'd said: he merely asked, quite mildly,

'If you were so worried about that, didn't it ever occur to you that you don't have to do what my grandmother wants? You could always have refused me, couldn't you? I suppose...it just wouldn't be...that you were afraid you wouldn't refuse me?' His hands tightened on her as she moved, and gave her a little shake. 'Answer me, Sara!'

'Oh—*damn* you, Paul Merinard!'

Her despairing glance did nothing more than make him laugh. 'That's what I wanted to know,' he said softly, and moved as if to start kissing her again. But then didn't. 'All right,' he said, 'I'll talk to you about Mylène. Not that you deserve it! I didn't know she'd been playing out one of her fantasies to justify her marital difficulties, and I certainly didn't know she'd involved me in it!'

'You're obviously very fond of her,' Sara flashed. Even against the pull of his nearness, and the weakness of loving him so much, she could remember the way that Paul had danced with Mylène—laughed with Mylène—

'Yes, of course I'm fond of her, she's my cousin and we grew up together! I was probably even in love with her once—when I was fourteen and she was seventeen!' Paul gave her a mocking look, then sobered. 'No, I must try and stop being angry with you, and be serious. If I'm gentle with Mylène, it's because I'm sorry for her. I know what her trouble is. Charles wants children. They've been trying to have them for years. Mylène's terrified that he'll leave her for that reason—not that he will, he may be extraordinarily dull, but he is devoted to her. She's a very neurotic lady, my cousin. Come to think of it, Charles really is the right man for her: it would take someone with an extremely placid temperament to bear living with her for long, let alone for the last eleven years! She'd drive me mad in a few weeks! But you, Sara—' he gave her a level look, 'you have to believe anything anyone ever tells you against me, don't you? Now, how am I going to cure you of that?'

'You mean it really isn't true—?'

'No, of course it isn't! Any more than it's true that I'm so obsessed with duty that I'd marry you just to please my grandmother,' Paul said with remarkable cheerfulness, and as if he hadn't felt Sara wince, started to laugh. 'You would have been in for a shock, wouldn't you—if you'd decided to be a sacrificial lamb—to find yourself with an unexpectedly devoted husband!'

'Paul—'

She was too breathless suddenly to say more

than his name. It might have been the way he was looking at her—smiling at her—with his eyes still gleaming with laughter. 'I should never have let you anywhere near grandmère,' he said, shaking his head, 'though I suppose, because she could see how besotted I seem to be with you, she thought she was trying to help. No, I should never have taken you there in the first place!'

'Why did you?'

'Would you believe, because I couldn't think of anywhere else to take you, and I couldn't bear the idea of letting you out of my sight? Mind you, if I'd known—' his hands were drawing her against him—'that between your hostility, and grandmère's sense of propriety, I was never going to be able to get anywhere near you... Oh, I'm forgetting something. I brought you this.'

He had half let her go, and was feeling in his pocket. The package he brought out was small and rectangular and as he unwrapped it Sara saw a white box with a line of gold round it. A—perfume box? He turned it round to face her and she saw the gold lettering on the front, very plain except for a curl on the initial letter. It said, 'Sara', and then, lower down on the box in much smaller letters,' 'Lorivel'.

'That was what I was going to take you Lorivel to show you, ten days ago,' he said, into her wide-eyed, disbelieving stare. 'Except that we hadn't got as far as printing the boxes then—you'd have had to see the design on the drawing-board. But if you don't like the idea it's too bad, because whether you marry me or not—and you *will*—you're going to find yourself seeing the name *"Sara de Lorivel"* staring back at you from a lot of magazine advertisements quite soon!'

'You—named your new perfume after *me*?'

'Who else would I name it after?' he asked softly—but with enough challenge edging his voice to stop her feeling dizzy for a moment so that she could bring out a retort.

'Well—Béatrice, or Linda, or Christine—wasn't it?'

'Oh, I'm glad you remember them so clearly. That shows I really did manage to make you jealous.' This time he did pull her close into his arms, taking the little box away as Sara reached for it, and putting it down on the floor beside them. 'No, you can't smell your sample bottle now, you can do that later. Because this is the first time I've managed to be properly alone with you since...and your friend's gone out, hasn't she? And I love you to distraction, my Sara, and I'm not very patient, so...'

She melted into his arms, answering the kisses which punctuated his words so willingly that he could never be in any doubt about whether she loved him. There didn't seem to be any need for any words at all, only a growing need in both of them which would soon be answered. And this time, there was no beginning in violence and temper and misunderstanding, only passion and magic, and a promise for the future.